A NEWPORT SUNRISE

CINDY NICHOLS

ONE

Mornings like this had a way of seeping right into Jen's soul. The ocean breeze —with a little chill as summer was long past —swept past her, and her toes dug in the sand on her way to the water.

Daisy, her puppy, led the way. The tug on the leash spurred them both on, and Jen let her mind wander as the salt spray of the waves cooled her cheeks. Daisy was content to splash while Jen sat on the sand, hugging her knees and thinking over how much her life had changed in the past months.

Even now, she sometimes couldn't believe how lucky she was. She'd fought long and hard to be here —watching the colors change over the ocean as the sun rose, something she could now do every day. Even the water changed color as the sun rose, or set.

It wasn't every day she was this grateful to watch the

sunrise. She'd never been much of a morning person, but Daisy had changed all that. A dog panting in her face at the first hint of light wasn't something she'd been able to ignore, so these days she saw more sunrises than she slept through.

She glanced up the beach toward Joe's house. Her stomach fluttered as she saw him walking toward her with a big smile, and she was reminded of one of the best parts of getting up this early —meeting him on the beach.

His dog, Boris, headed straight for Daisy as Jen gratefully accepted the to-go cup of coffee Joe held out to her.

"I was hoping you'd bring this. Your mom makes the best," Jen said as she inhaled the rich aroma of the coffee.

Joe sat down beside her in the sand and nodded. "I hate to admit that you may be right. But don't tell her. It'll go to her head."

Jen laughed, knowing that wasn't true. Mrs. Russo was good at everything in the kitchen, but wasn't the least bit vain about it. It was just a fact. Her Italian food was the foundation of their gondola business in the harbor — people came as much for the food as the ride.

"How's my favorite gondolier?" Jen asked, picturing him in his red and white striped shirt, black pants and straw hat. It always made her smile.

Joe rubbed his biceps. "I'm getting a little old for the actual work. Happy to run the books while Ma does the food, but this old body isn't cut out for paddling people around all night. Good thing I only have to when one of the younger guys calls in sick. Last night's trip was a proposal, and I didn't want to cancel. Wouldn't want anybody to miss out on eternal happiness or anything."

Jen blew on her coffee and took a sip. "What a romantic you are. That's very sweet."

"Gotta support people being happy," he said. "I was sorry to cancel dinner last night, though."

"I'm sorry, too. I missed you, but happy to sacrifice in the name of love."

And not for the first time, Jen realized that she meant it —she really had missed him. It wasn't just that she was alone. She'd spent lots of time alone, and it didn't bother her. No, she had to admit that she really missed his company. At least admit it to herself. And if she was able to admit it to herself, it was probably time to admit it to her best friends, Faith and Carrie.

"I guess I won't see you tonight, either, since it's Friday night happy hour with the girls."

"Right," Jen said softly. She was excited to see Faith and Carrie later that evening, as usual, for their weekly ritual but also had that tug in her heart, sorry she wouldn't be seeing Joe, too. It was only a vaguely familiar feeling — one she hadn't felt for many, many years. Her husband had been gone for so long that she'd almost forgotten what it felt like.

But it was becoming more clear by the day. She

thanked her lucky stars that they'd been able to rekindle the friendship they'd fostered so long ago, when they were younger.

"What've you got going today?" he asked as they sipped their coffee and the dogs bounded through the waves. They didn't seem to notice at all that the water had also gotten cooler along with the breeze.

"I've spent most of the week going through more of Nana's things."

"I hope it's nothing like my dad's room. I'm not going to finish with that before the end of the year."

Jen laughed and knew he was right. She'd been in that room, and it was filled floor-to-ceiling with knick-knacks, some of which were pretty valuable. But it took a lot of time to find out what was what.

"No, this is more normal stuff. Some cookbooks, more clothes. It's fun to see what's in there, but I don't expect anything too unusual."

Joe stood and reached his hand out for Jen, helping her up.

"Never know," he said. "Sounds fun. Wish I could join you, but it's end of month for the business, and I've got to work on the books."

Jen nodded and called for Daisy. "Come on up to the house before you go. I've got some leftovers for you from last night."

Joe's eyes lit up. "Wow, thanks. That's nice of you after I stood you up."

Jen headed up toward the house and smiled. "I think we're beyond that, aren't we? I didn't feel stood up. I knew we'd have another opportunity."

Joe tugged on Jen's elbow and stopped her, turning her toward him. The sun was up over the horizon now, and the sun sparkled on the waves in the crisp autumn breeze.

"I'm glad you know that. That we'll have another opportunity."

Jen looked into his eyes, and her stomach fluttered again. "I do. And it makes me happy."

"Me, too," he said as he leaned forward, softly resting his lips on hers.

She closed her eyes and relished the feeling —one more thing that she hadn't felt in many, many years. And had forgotten how much she enjoyed.

When he pulled away, she sighed and glanced at the sand before she looked up into his eyes once more.

"That was nice," she said.

He nodded and smiled wide. "It was."

Joe held his arm out and she looped her arm through his. They walked quietly up to the house, and she couldn't think of a single thing to say —she just felt comfortable and happy.

They reached the house, and she squeezed his arm after he let them both in the gate. The dogs set to rolling on the small patch of grass, and Jen grabbed the leftovers from the refrigerator.

She handed him the bag and he raised his eyebrows.

"I missed homemade enchiladas?"

She smiled and nodded. "They'll be just as good for you and your mom tonight."

"The company won't be as good, that's for sure." He smiled and planted a kiss on her cheek. He called for Boris and looked around the garden. He picked up some roof shingles and said, "I'm only an accountant, but I'm pretty sure roof shingles are supposed to stay on the roof."

"Oh, man. They must have blown off last night in the wind," Jen said as she took them from him and looked up. Sure enough, there were a few empty spots over the awning.

"Guess I'll be looking for a contractor. That's not something I want to head into winter with."

Joe nodded. "I could patch it, but you should definitely get a roofer out to see how bad it is."

"Oh, thanks. I really appreciate it. I'll start looking around for somebody. Come for dinner tomorrow? Faith will be here, and we could invite Carrie and Dirk."

"Sounds great," he said. He lifted the bag of leftovers and backed out the gate. "I'm a lucky man."

Jen watched him head up the boardwalk. He turned around and waved before he turned the corner toward his house, and Jen knew she was a lucky woman, too.

TWO

It seemed a normal end to a normal kindergarten school day when, suddenly, everything in Faith's world stopped.

"No, Jason, don't," she'd cried, to no avail. Time slowed as the five-year-old picked up the hamster cage, his ear-to-ear grin full of excitement.

And somehow, in her teacher's heart with decades of experience, she knew what was going to happen next.

He turned toward her and began to run, almost immediately tripping over his own feet.

The hamster cage flew through the air and she ran toward it, doing her best imitation of a wide receiver in a life or death football game.

Her breath whooshed as she landed on her back, the intact hamster cage thudding on her chest. She blinked several times, amazed that the only damage was having the breath knocked out of her.

"I'm sorry, Mrs. Donovan. I didn't mean to —"

Faith waved him off with a thin smile, and as soon as she caught her breath and could speak, she said, "It's okay, Jason. But remember, we are not supposed to pick up the hamster cage."

It was a hard and fast rule in her kindergarten classroom —but one that was broken almost daily. She couldn't count the times she'd had to get a new cage this school year, and it was still not even Thanksgiving. Not to mention that she'd become a pro at chasing down the darn thing when it was either let out or escaped.

Jason had recovered more quickly than Faith had herself.

"Mrs. Donovan, can I take the hamster home for the weekend?"

Not a week went by without one of Faith's kindergarten students asking to take the hamster home, or the basil plants, or the goldfish. She'd always said no, but now as she peered into the cage at the hamster, who was staring back at her and wiggling its whiskers, she was sorely tempted to break her own rule.

Faith ignored the creaking in her knees as she knelt down in front of the cute little boy.

"Jason, we've talked about this, and I have to say no. I really appreciate you wanting to help, but he's used to being here in the classroom."

"I'll take really good care of Jack. I promise. My mom said she would help me."

Faith looked up to see his mother's smiling, hopeful face in the doorway, and she returned the friendly wave. "I know she would, Jason. But you know we need to keep him here. He's too little for a sleepover."

His crestfallen face tugged at her heart, but after several decades of experience with this, she knew the odds of getting any of the pets —or plants —back intact was slim to zero. As evidenced by her very recent experience of the poor hamster flying through the air.

The next few minutes were like a tornado as the students ended yet another week in her classroom. It was getting close to Thanksgiving vacation so the energy level was a little frenetic. Only a few more weeks and they'd all have a break. And she knew she needed one.

She gathered up her things in the quiet room, and sat down behind her desk. The squeaking of her old chair didn't deter Faith from leaning back anyway after the last kindergartner closed the door behind him at the end of her Friday. The loud, familiar squeak somehow soothed her as she rocked back and forth. She wondered how many times that day she'd been able to sneak a moment in it while her charges were occupied —not many. She rubbed her closed eyes and took a deep breath.

Friday. At least it was Friday. And she couldn't wait to be on the deck at the beach house with Jen and Carrie. She was amazed she hadn't missed even one, in all these weeks that she'd been teaching school during the week and traveling to the beach on the weekends.

But the cost had been a little higher than she'd envisioned. She got up with the sunrise and rarely hit the hay before midnight, falling into her comfy bed completely exhausted. Between her job as a kindergarten teacher, her other job at the boutique on the weekends, her pillow-design hobby and all the prep work that went along with teaching, the only thing she'd had to cut time from was sleep. And she was feeling it.

Her daughter, Maggy, called to check on her most every night, and Faith looked forward to that —mostly. The last time they'd talked, though, Faith wondered if maybe it was better if they didn't talk so frequently.

"Mom, you sound tired."

Faith had mustered her best, lightest laugh. "I'm fine, honey. Just a lot to do, with school and the boutique."

Maggy had paused for a moment, and Faith gripped her phone a little tighter.

"Just so you aren't burning the candle at both ends. You know it's not good for you to be stressed."

Well, there it was. Her daughter was worried...again. Whenever Faith got even close to doing too much, it brought back memories for Maggy. No matter how much Faith had tried over the years to allay her fears, they never stayed gone for long.

But there wasn't much she could do about it now, except say what she always said.

"I'm fine, honey. You don't need to worry about me."

All of that had been long ago, and Faith had learned a lot about keeping things on an even keel for herself. But if she was honest, these last long weeks had made her wonder what had happened to all her stamina.

Like she'd said to Maggy, though, she was fine, and just needed to keep swimming and keep her head above water. At least for another school year. Maybe two.

Besides, worrying was her job and shouldn't be her daughter's. And she was a pro at it. She'd been born a worrier, and so she had decades of practice. She had it down to a science, from worrying about her students after they'd gone home to poring over her meager budget. And of course, worrying about Maggy. She'd always considered it part of her job —as a teacher, as a mom, as a friend and, previously, as a wife.

Lord knew her ex-husband had given her plenty to worry about. At least that part was in the past now.

The last thing Maggy had said, "You need to have some fun. Promise me," had made Faith laugh outright. The only fun she allowed herself to have was the weekends at the beach house. At least she had that —and Carrie and Jen.

She rolled her heavy shoulders a few times, ignoring the crackling, then filled her tote bag with the things she'd need over the weekend. Thankfully, she'd been teaching kindergarten for enough years that she'd honed her lesson plans and didn't need to do much with those except tweak them for the different personalities in her classroom. And there sure were a lot of personalities. She smiled at the thought of Quinn, who refused to wear anything but dresses and seemed undaunted by the skinned knees that her attire allowed during recess when she also refused to let the boys keep her from a good game of dodge ball.

She chuckled at the thought of Thomas and his future best friend, Alex, who'd held hands on their way in the door on the first day of school after they'd only just met. Now fast friends, they'd somehow decided to become "class helpers," strongly encouraging the others to fall in line and follow the rules. She was grateful for all the different personalities, both the easy ones and the challenging ones.

But as they were home with their parents for the weekend, she'd do her best to fully immerse herself in the soothing sound of the waves and the warm breeze on her cheeks at the beach with her best friends. At least until she had to go work at the boutique the next day.

The phone on her desk buzzed, and since the class was empty, she put the intercom on speaker.

"Faith here," she said, wondering why there were still people in the office. Usually the entire place cleared out pretty quickly on a Friday afternoon —she joked, but sometimes it felt like the grown-ups running for their lives.

"Hi, Faith, it's Amy. I know it's Friday, and it's been a

long week. Thought maybe you'd forgotten about the retirement briefing in the teachers' lounge."

Faith closed her eyes, and her forehead dropped into her hand. "Oh, gosh, I did. Thanks, Amy. I'll be right there."

She clicked off the intercom and thanked her lucky stars that Amy was one of the best principals she'd ever worked with. She was thoughtful like that —reminding people about things that would help them. Retirement was still a ways off for her, but it never hurt to get as much information as possible.

She grabbed her tote bag and took a glance around the room. Jack had enough food and water for the weekend, but she leaned over the cage anyway and blew him a kiss.

"I'll be back before you know it, little guy," she said before she clicked off the lights, locked the door and headed to the teacher's lounge.

THREE

"You look tired," Amy said when Faith rushed into the lounge and took a seat in the back.

"Thanks," Faith said with a laugh. Her principal had never been one to pull punches, but that one stung a bit. Faith knew she'd been running at a pretty fast clip for weeks, but she still had her head above water.

The presenter from the district's personnel office had begun to drone on with information Faith had heard at least a thousand times —or at least it felt like that many. She knew the numbers. She knew the union contract. She knew she couldn't retire yet. Yet she sat in the required meeting anyway.

"Could you step outside for a minute? I have something I want to ask you?" Amy whispered.

Faith nodded and followed her principal out the door.

"What's up?" Faith asked, wanting to know as soon as possible. She didn't like surprises.

"I have a line on someone who didn't sign a contract in September, but is willing to for the second half of the year, starting in January. She's great. A real find."

Faith knew how difficult it was to compete for new teachers —especially good ones. And Amy knew good ones when she saw them. It would be great for the elementary school that Faith had dedicated decades to and it was one of the things she admired most about Amy.

"I know you're not ready to retire, and please don't take this the wrong way but I thought maybe you might appreciate a helping hand. If I want to hire her, I need to grab her right away. I have budget to offer her a student teaching position for the rest of this semester, and I thought maybe you'd like to have her with you."

"Oh," Faith said slowly. "Am I losing it? Do I need a babysitter?"

Amy laughed and held up her hands. "I was afraid you'd think that. That's absolutely not the case. I just thought of you first. I'm sure lots of people would love the help. You know how that is. She's a great find, excellent teacher, and in addition, she could really benefit from your experience and organizational skills. Not to mention your expertise in handling the little ones."

Faith felt a little bit better after, and let out a sigh of

relief. She actually could use the help, and if Amy thought highly of this teacher it was a safe bet.

They talked over the particulars and agreed she'd start on Monday, and Faith tried to stay awake through the rest of the presentation by thinking how excited she was to get to the beach house.

She hurried home to change and grabbed the clothes she'd laid out earlier when she packed. She tugged on her favorite beach pants and sighed.

Faith tugged at the zipper one more time, thinking maybe one last pull might do it. These weren't even her skinny jeans, and it took a while for her to admit defeat.

She wriggled out of the capris and tossed them onto the chair in her bedroom. She could swear that they'd fit fine last week when she pulled them on to head to the beach house for the weekend. Could she have gained that much weight in just a week that she couldn't zip up her favorites?

As she rummaged in her closet, it occurred to her that maybe it had been more than a week since she'd worn those. The weeks were going by so fast, what with being back in the classroom with her kindergartners and spending every weekend down in Newport, working at the boutique. Maybe she hadn't worn them in a while after all.

Still. She grudgingly turned to the "other" section of her closet, the one with the next size up. Like most everybody else she knew, she had probably three sizes for different times of her life, but she hadn't wanted to visit this size again.

The elastic waist slid right up when she pulled them on, and she rolled her eyes even though she was alone. "No more potato chips for you," she said out loud —again, to no one.

The new information required that she quickly re-sort her weekend bag with clothes from "that" section. She made sure to leave the bathing suit she wouldn't be wearing, but she made quick work of it and headed downstairs.

She'd packed a small ice chest with things she didn't want to let go bad while she was gone, and as a last thought, she took the box of small potato chip bags that had sat on her counter for a couple weeks and tossed them in. Maybe they had been too easy to grab and she could pawn them off on Jen and Carrie. They were always skinny — their weight didn't seem to bounce up and down like her own. They could handle them.

The pillows that she'd made this past week were already in her ancient Toyota, so this was her last load. When she'd first gone back to school, she'd left her sewing machines at the beach house. She'd quickly found herself at loose ends, though, so she'd brought them home and made more pillows when she could spare the time.

Which wasn't all that often, but it was a nice creative outlet for her. She spent hours on designing them, adding beads or appliqués, sometimes hand-sewing on sequins or delicate little mirrors. She loved it, and it helped her forget about all the other things she was doing.

As she got on the freeway, her old car vibrating more than it should when she tried to get to the beach house as quickly as she could, she caught the last part of the news.

"ANOTHER WINDY WEEKEND, with fire danger off the charts..."

"GREAT." Faith clicked off the radio. Fire season in Southern California had been getting worse and worse in the past few years, it seemed. She made a mental note to mention it to Jen —it was much less windy down at the beach, but with all the eucalyptus trees at Jen's house inland, fire was always a worry. She'd had some close calls in the past.

The traffic wasn't too bad for a Friday, and the temperature had dropped considerably by the time she turned onto the Newport peninsula. The temperature gauge in her old car had risen during the drive, so she slowed down, turned the A/C off and rolled down the windows.

The salty, cooler air swept through the car and she almost felt like she'd been transported to another place — but of course she had been.

She glanced toward the passenger seat at the retirement brochures that peeked out of her tote bag. There was no way she could afford to retire yet, although she'd give anything to be down in Newport full time with Jen and Carrie.

She reached over and tucked the paperwork down into her bag so it wouldn't mock her. Passing Carrie's dental office, she noticed that Carrie's convertible wasn't in the parking lot. The girls were probably waiting for her, glasses in hand as they watched the sunset from the deck.

She threw caution to the wind and sped up, not wanting to waste a moment of the precious time she did have at the beach. She was ready to get the weekend started.

FOUR

Jen's brief encounter with Joe earlier had reminded her that it was Friday, her favorite day of the week —the day Faith would head down from her job inland. Jen was busy enough during the week just going through Nana's things —she was surprised how much was left even after she and Faith and Carrie had gone through everything for the fashion show a few weeks earlier. But when she really thought about it, a life well-lived for over ninety years was bound to accumulate some interesting things.

And some of the things she'd found were extremely interesting. As she went through the many boxes up in the annex filled with scrapbooks, pictures, jewelry, knick-knacks —it was fairly frequent that she'd glance at her watch and hours had gone by as she learned more and more about her beloved grandmother.

One of the things she found that surprised her was an

old recipe book dated from the 1940s. It wasn't one that had been published, and when she first flipped through it, she'd wondered whose handwriting it was. On the very last page, she'd found an inscription:

TO MY NEW DAUGHTER-IN-LAW. In these pages are all of my son's favorite recipes to start you off right as you leave for California. Welcome to the family.

JEN HAD TURNED it gently over in her hands, her mind traveling back to the Midwest during that time. It would have been right before World War II, and many of recipes were quite basic and simple. But if Nana hadn't known how to cook at all back then, it would have been invaluable. And as she looked at it more closely, many of the pages were worn and tattered, with the regular splotches of oil or butter that adorned her own favorite cookbooks.

She tucked that one in the stack that she intended to keep, separating it from other things that seemed less meaningful. She'd planned to take as much as she could to the vintage store, but as she glanced around the room she realized that the stacks she wanted to keep were much bigger than the ones she planned to donate.

She finally ended her trip through Nana's world and

realized she'd better get started if she wanted to pull off her plan. The cookbook she'd set aside was on the kitchen island, and she laughed as she glanced at some of the things she'd tried during the week just for entertainment. She wasn't at all sure how the girls were going to feel about what she'd made —but she was fairly positive they weren't going to oooh and aaah over the spicy pickled beets that Nana's mother-in-law said were her son's favorite. Jen had just finished tidying up the beach house when her phone buzzed.

I FORGOT about a staff meeting after school. I'll be a little late. Darn!

JEN WAS DEFINITELY disappointed when she read the text, but knew it must be important, because Faith was looking forward to coming down as much as Jen was looking forward to Faith's arrival.

If Faith still wasn't on the road, Jen probably had time to take Daisy for a walk. A good one, which she hadn't had in a while. Jen wasn't much of an early riser, and when Daisy panted in her face at the crack of dawn, all she had energy for was a quick walk before the coffee pot called her name and brought her back to the porch.

But if she had a little extra time, it might be a good

opportunity to give her a little more exercise. And maybe they'd run into Boris and Joe, if they were lucky.

Jen was grateful for Joe and Mrs. Russo, and usually stopped by to chat when she could. The dogs loved to play on the small plot of grass outside Joe's beachfront home, and Mrs. Russo was always fun to hear from.

But Joe had turned into a very good friend. He'd always been a good friend to Jen and her late husband, but since they'd been able to spend time together after Joe moved back to Newport from Chicago, it was as if Jen was getting to know him all over again. Getting to know the Joe he was now —and sharing with him a Jen much different than the young girl he'd known before they each married and moved away.

She'd purposely not mentioned to either Faith or Carrie that he'd been spending a couple of evenings a week at the beach house, having dinner and watching design shows afterward while the puppies played.

Jen told herself that Daisy needed Boris's company, and it had only been recently that she'd admitted to herself that she enjoyed Joe's company as much as she did. And after this morning —when he kissed her —it was probably time to talk about it. She never really did know what was going to come up during their Friday night get-togethers, but this would be a doozy.

FIVE

"She's here!"

Jen rushed down the stairs and out the front door, Carrie right behind her. Jen gave Faith a big hug, as did Carrie, but she paused for a minute as she stepped back and took a look at Faith.

"Wow, Faith. You look, um..."

Faith glanced down at her waist, and her cheeks flushed. "I know. I've gained a little weight. I was hoping you wouldn't notice."

Jen shook her head and frowned. "No, it's not that. You're fine. We all go up and down."

Jen reached for the bag Faith held out before she turned to get the rest of her things out of the car. Jen peered inside and laughed.

"Where did you get all these potato chips?"

Faith shook her head. "I think that's part of the problem. Maggy sent me a whole box of them, and of course I seem to grab one every time I pass by the bowl I put them in. Can't help myself. You guys need to eat the rest."

"Happy to help with that," Carrie said. She grabbed some things from Faith and they took the load upstairs to Faith's bedroom.

"Ah, thanks," Faith said, plopping down on a deck chair. "Quicker with all three of us."

Carrie handed Faith a glass of wine, and Jen still hadn't pinpointed exactly why Faith looked a little different. It really wasn't the weight, although it wasn't the thinnest she'd seen her friend of thirty years. No, it was something else.

"How was work this week?" Carrie asked, and they all laughed as Faith recounted the story of Jack, the hamster.

"You should have brought him down. He would have fit right in around here," Jen said.

"I may have to for the Thanksgiving holiday. I'm not sure he'd survive that long without me, and I can't trust any of those kindergarteners."

Carrie finished her bag of potato chips and reached for another one. "I see what you mean about these. They're addicting."

"I know, and there are three flavors. It's been a nightmare."

Jen nodded toward the sour cream and onion flavor

Carrie held up, and caught it perfectly when Carrie tossed it across the deck.

"Why did Maggy send you all of these?"

"Oh, she was having some friends over after volleyball and I helped her plan a menu. You know, since she's realized she's allergic to wheat it's been hard. She wanted to do barbecued chicken sandwiches but not make a big deal about not being able to eat the bun, so I suggested potato chips and she could just dip them in the barbecued chicken. I said it sounded really good and I'd make it myself, except I didn't have any barbecue sauce or potato chips, for that matter. Next day, a big Amazon box arrived on my doorstop with both. She said that was the smallest amount she could find. And I've been paying for it ever since," Faith said, tugging at the elastic waistband of her sweatpants.

"Aw, that was really sweet of her. She's so thoughtful," Jen said as she polished off the small bag of chips.

"She is, but sometimes the thought is better than the reality," Faith said, wiggling her eyebrows as she reached for a bag of chips. "How's Bethany?"

Carrie nodded and smiled. "She's good. She's done with tennis season, but we play pretty regularly after school. She's away this weekend at a tennis camp. Said she doesn't want to lose her edge. She's being scouted already, and she really wants a tennis scholarship."

Faith whistled. "Wow, that's impressive. And I'm glad you guys are having fun."

Carrie held out her empty wine glass when Jen lifted the bottle to offer refills.

A strong gust of wind swept across the deck, and Carrie grabbed the stack of napkins before they took flight.

"Oh, I meant to tell you. On the radio they said that there are supposed to be pretty big Santa Ana winds this weekend. Just wanted to let you know. I don't think they'll be too bad down here, but I was thinking of all the eucalyptus trees back at the house."

"Shoot. Really?" Jen's stomach dropped at the words. They'd had so many close calls with wildfires over the years, and now she wouldn't be there in case there was fire close by. "Maybe I should go spend the weekend, just in case," she said, although she really didn't want to. She looked toward the waves crashing against the beach and remembered that this weekend was supposed to be a particularly high tide.

"I know you worry about the house, but that would be awful if you had to go. Well, not awful, and I don't mean to make it all about me, but I've been really looking forward to a break. I need you guys. I'm tired."

Jen snapped her fingers the second Faith said that. "That's it. You look tired." She hadn't quite been able to put her finger on it. It wasn't as if Faith had dark circles under her eyes or anything, but she definitely looked —well, maybe weary was the right word.

"Thanks," Faith said with a laugh. "Between having to change into bigger sweats and that compliment, I'm feeling pretty lovely."

Jen nudged her arm. "I don't mean it in a bad way. I really just want to know if you're all right."

Carrie leaned forward in her chair. "Yeah, you really are doing a lot. Working during the week and on the weekends, and all the pillows."

Faith nodded slowly. "I know. I really am a little tired. Just trying to hang in there until Thanksgiving, and we only have a couple of weeks to go. I'll be fine. And Amy got me a student teacher, so that should help a lot."

Jen cocked her head and studied her long-time friend. "Well, that's good but I still think you're trying to do too much. I hate to use the 'R' word."

Carrie's eyes widened, and she looked from Jen to Faith.

Faith held up her hand and stopped Jen's train of thought. "I actually was late today because they had a retirement seminar after school. Why they'd do that on a Friday afternoon, I don't know."

"And?" Jen asked, her eyebrows raised.

Faith leaned back in her chair and hugged her knees. "It confirmed for me that I've got a few more years to go. I can't afford to retire yet, no matter how tired I am."

"Darn. I was hoping you could move down here with me and just work at the boutique on the weekends."

"That would be fantastic. Maybe in a few years."

"Not even if you sell your house?" Carrie asked. Jen shot her a look, but it was too late. Jen could only think that Carrie didn't remember that Faith had had to mortgage it to the hilt to put Maggy through college, after what her ex, Jeff, had done.

Carrie flushed and looked down at her orange sandals. "Oh, right. Sorry, I forgot."

Jen cleared her throat. "I hate to mention it, but have you considered quitting at the boutique? I know you enjoy it, but maybe you need to back up a little bit. You can't stay this stressed for this long."

Faith closed her eyes and rubbed her forehead. "Honestly, I don't get paid much there, but I've been putting away every little bit. Putting it toward the mortgage so that maybe if I ever can sell it, I'll get a little out of it."

Jen sighed and looked out at the crashing waves, wishing she could help. The sun had just set, and she watched for the green flash as she always did. Both Carrie and Faith watched, too.

"Nothing?" Carrie asked.

"Nope, not me," Faith said.

"Me, neither," Jen added. "Wow, the wind's really picking up. You guys ready for dinner? Well, appetizers, really. I found an old cookbook of Nana's, from her then new mother-in-law. We're having appetizers from the forties."

"What? Really?" Faith asked. "What did they eat for appetizers back then?"

Jen winked at them and laughed. "You'll see. Follow me, ladies. I promise it won't kill you."

SIX

Jen was tempted to get her phone and take a video of Faith and Carrie as they looked at the spread on the table. It was quite comical —Faith looked a little more interested than Carrie did. Carrie just looked scared.

"What —what are these things?" Carrie finally asked, pointing at the plate of purple slimy things.

Jen held up Nana's cookbook she'd found. "Those, my dear, are pickled beets. Apparently, it was my grandfather's favorite."

"Ugh, really?" Faith asked.

Jen flipped to the end of the book. "Well, that's what her mother-in-law said, but Nana made a note in here from 1960. It's hilarious."

"ROBERT FINALLY TOLD me the truth. I made pickled

beets for his birthday —for the twentieth time. His mother told me it was his favorite, but today he told me he couldn't stand it. Never wanted to tell his mother, and hadn't wanted to tell me either. We both got quite the laugh out of it. I'd rip it out of the book, but it should stay for posterity."

CARRIE BURST OUT LAUGHING. "Typical marriage. Takes almost twenty years to tell the truth."

Jen wondered about that. She and Allen had only been married for five years before he passed away. And she thought that now, with Joe —they told each other the truth even now, at the beginning. At least she hoped they did.

Faith pulled out a chair and passed around the appetizer plates. "Hm. The truth I got after twenty years —well, it wasn't pretty."

"Yeah, but better late than never," Carrie said. "And besides, once you knew, you could act. You actually got to rip the page out of the book."

Faith laughed. "I guess you're right. Like ripping off a Band-Aid."

Jen thought about Jeff, and what he'd done to Faith and Maggy. She had always been impressed that Faith had done so well with it.

"Faith, you really handled all that smoothly, for how awful it was. It was like ripping off a Band-Aid, but you did it. And you did it well."

Faith shook her head. "Maybe, but that was after the first phone call I made. To you. Remember?"

Jen patted Faith's hand at the memory. "You couldn't breathe, couldn't get the words out. I wasn't sure what had happened. I first thought somebody had died."

Faith reached for a pimento-cheese-stuffed piece of celery. "I know. I'm sorry. I literally had the breath knocked out of me when I got the call."

Jen remembered how hard it had been and wouldn't wish on any wife to find out her husband had a girlfriend, had taken her to your mountain cabin and on top of that, was telling friends on Facebook that they were in bed watching Netflix movies. On your own Netflix account. That you paid for.

"Actually, in hindsight, it was a good thing he got drunk enough to post all of that online. Otherwise, you may never have found out."

Faith raised her eyebrows and nodded approvingly as she bit into the miniature chicken pot pies and Jen was relieved at least they liked something on the table. "I might not have agreed with you at the time, but I do now. Thanks for talking me off the ledge. First of many times you had to."

"I don't agree. I think you handled it remarkably well after you found out. That was it. It was done," Carrie said, her nose crinkled. She leaned forward and gingerly poked her fork into the colorful gelatin mold she'd tried. "What the heck is this?"

Jen pushed the plate closer to Carrie, and laughed when she actually recoiled. "Don't be a wuss. It's Jell-O. It's not as bad as it looks. It was brand new then."

Carrie didn't look entirely convinced, but put some on her plate anyway.

"I'm just glad it's all ancient history. Relationships are hard," Faith said.

Carrie nodded in agreement. "No kidding. I was happy to see the back side of Rob, too."

The wave of emotion surprised Jen, and she set her fork down and leaned back in her chair. She watched her friends giggle and chat about the different kinds of foods, and she filled in the information she had when they asked about something in particular. But she'd lost her appetite. Her marriage experience had been very different, and obviously she wasn't at all happy when hers ended.

She'd thought about talking to them about Joe, but all of a sudden it didn't seem like quite as good an idea.

They finished sampling appetizers and there were clear winners and losers. The plate that had held pot pies was empty, but the Jell-O mold ring was almost still a complete circle.

"Well, that wasn't nearly as scary as I anticipated." Carrie stood and reached for the empty plates.

"Not bad at all," Faith agreed. She reached for the leftovers to take to the kitchen and stopped as the wind whistled through the windows. "It's sure howling out tonight. Glad we left the deck when we did."

Jen walked around the room, securing the windows. They were old and drafty, and sometimes they even flew open with a strong enough breeze. If the howling outside at the moment was any indication what the night might hold, it was better to batten down the hatches.

"I can only imagine how hard it's blowing inland," she said, sure that her voice was tinged with the worry she was feeling.

Faith set the dishes in the sink and began to fill the sink to wash them. "Hey, I have an idea."

Jen followed them into the kitchen, reaching for containers to put the leftovers in. "What?"

"Why don't you ask Michael and Amber if they want to spend the weekend at the house? They're in that tiny apartment, anyway. They might enjoy going, right?"

Jen rubbed her temples. "This will sound awful. Once Max told me he was going to stay in Boston for the fall and do another internship round, and I came to terms with the fact he wouldn't be staying at the house, I completely forgot that Michael and Amber could stay there."

"Oops," Faith said with a laugh.

"I know. I'm a horrible mother. And a horrible mother-in-law. And a horrible grandmother-to-be."

"Whoa. Stop. They could have asked. Just call and ask them. Quit beating yourself up."

Jen nodded. "Okay, I will. That's a great idea, Faith. I was thinking anyway —this week is supposed to be an especially high tide and with the wind it'll be even worse. Not to mention the roof shingles I found in the garden after the last high winds. And I can't be in both places at once."

They finished the dishes and sat down in the living room —it was way too windy to go outside. Faith dropped out of the conversation pretty quickly, and Carrie and Jen soon realized that their friend had fallen fast asleep.

"Wow, she's really burning the candle at both ends," Jen whispered. She pulled a quilt from the closet as Carrie tucked the softest pillow on the couch under Faith's head.

Jen spread the quilt over her friend while Carrie took off Faith's shoes and set them to the side of the couch. They tiptoed outside, taking Daisy with them.

Jen looked over her shoulder at the sleeping Faith. "I hope she's okay."

"She seems all right. I mean, it would be better if she had more time on her hands and could have some fun, relax a little, but she seems to be holding up pretty well."

Jen nodded. "We'll just have to keep an eye on her."

"Yep. Thanks for dinner and I'll call you guys tomorrow."

Jen waved just before Carrie turned the corner on the

way to her condo and the wind had died down a little bit. She sat on the stoop while Daisy considered whether or not to do her business.

With impeccable timing, Daisy finished her mission right as the wind picked back up again and, as quietly as possible, Jen grabbed her phone, turned off the lights and headed upstairs to call Michael and Amber, and see if they might be interested in staying at the house for the weekend. That would take at least one item off her worry list, and she could focus on what was right in front of her. Faith and the rising tide.

SEVEN

Faith was dreaming of fire-breathing dragons when her eyes flew open. It took her a little while to realize that it wasn't a dragon breathing in her face but Daisy, the border collie puppy.

And that she wasn't in her bedroom upstairs but on the couch downstairs with a blanket over her, and that she wasn't in her pajamas.

She vaguely recalled lying down on the couch while Carrie and Jen were chatting, and she remembered trying very hard to listen to what Jen was saying about Michael and Amber But she didn't remember at all what they actually had decided, and the next thing she knew —she had a dog breathing in her face.

She was also positive that she hadn't had too much wine. She rarely did that, especially after her experience with Jeff. Since she had to be up and running every day so early, she made an extra special point of it, even on weekends.

She gave up trying to remember, though, and sat up and stretched.

Daisy hopped on the couch next to Faith and rested her head on Faith's lap. It was early —very early —and she knew this time of the morning wasn't Jen's favorite. Maybe she'd appreciate a break from the early morning dog walk.

She slipped on her tennis shoes that she didn't remember taking off, started a pot of coffee and grabbed Daisy's leash.

The cool morning air went a long way toward blowing the cobwebs out of Faith's head as Daisy pulled them toward the beach. She'd grabbed a sweater as closer to the holidays the mornings were more brisk than balmy, and she was glad she had. Even Daisy wasn't as eager as she used to be to splash in the waves, and they were both content to just walk along the shoreline.

After her experience the day before with her jeans, she picked up the pace. She was happy to have Daisy's exuberance spur her on and before she knew it, she was all the way to the pier. It was still pretty early, but Dory's fish market was doing a brisk business. She wondered if many of the people she saw there were buying for restaurants, and wished she'd brought her wallet to bring something back for Jen to cook, or Carrie to barbecue.

She would next time, for sure. She spotted an empty

bench and decided to catch her breath for a minute. Daisy's pace wasn't Faith's normal slow one, but hopefully it would help her get back in her skinnier jeans.

She watched the people at the market for a little bit and as she usually did, wondered what fish markets were like in other places. She'd always wanted to travel, and had often wondered what it would be like to visit small markets around the world. What did they sell in markets in Italy? In France? She really would love to see. She wasn't as good a cook as Jen, but she loved to try new things, new tastes, new spices.

She took another look at the people around. Walkers of all kinds —couples of all ages, people walking alone, and lots of dogs.

"Penny for your thoughts," a man said as he sat down beside her, and when she saw Daisy's tail wagging and Boris's wiggling just as fast, she knew it was Joe.

"Hi," she said with a big smile as he gave her a hug.

Joe smiled and nodded. "Hello. Nice to see you. And Daisy, of course."

"Of course," Faith said. "And my thoughts were traveling the globe, sampling exotic wares in small markets. About as close to a real vacation as I'm going to get. How have you been? What's new and exciting?"

Joe rubbed his chin, his dark eyes thoughtful. "I guess I would say yes. The gondola business is getting under control, and of course isn't quite as busy as it was during the summer. I'm enjoying the extra time."

"I bet you are. I'm jealous," Faith said.

He cocked his head and turned toward her. "Jealous?"

Faith took a moment to explain her schedule and by the time she was finished, he was rubbing the back of his neck.

"Wow, I'm tired just hearing about it. Any relief in sight?"

"No," was on the tip of Faith's tongue, but she remembered that Thanksgiving break was right around the corner.

"I guess so. A little while until Thanksgiving. That'll be nice."

"Right. It sure will be," he agreed. "It's a pretty busy week for gondola trips because everybody's out of school and on vacation. We'll flip roles."

"I guess so," Faith said, looking forward to the particular role she would get to take.

"That'll be nice for Jen to have you around, particularly during that week when I won't be able to come over so much. It'll be great."

Faith blinked a few times, surprised by that information. Come over so much? Clearly, Jen had been holding out on her.

"It's great you've been able to spend so much time

together," she said, hoping she wasn't fishing for information too hard but dying to find out more.

"It's been really nice. Jen is —well, she's special. I love anything we do together. Just having dinner, watching house flipping shows, whatever. Doesn't matter. I just love her company."

"Huh," was all Faith could think of to say. Boy, would Jen be getting some questions as soon as Faith saw her.

But it wouldn't be all that soon. "I've got to run if I'm going to get to the boutique on time. Great to see you, and I hope I'll see you again this weekend."

"You will. Jen invited me for dinner tonight, and I look forward to it."

"Ah, great," Faith said. "That'll be fun. See you then."

She had to tug hard to get Daisy to leave Boris, but it eventually worked and she walked as fast as she could back toward the house. She was thrilled for her friend, and couldn't believe she'd have to wait to get more details. It was almost more than she could stand, but it wouldn't do to be late to her second job.

EIGHT

Jen couldn't believe her eyes when she woke up and glanced at the clock on the nightstand. It had been months since she'd slept in this late —well, ever since she inherited Daisy.

She pulled herself out of bed and was met with the aroma of coffee wafting up the stairs. Thank goodness for Faith.

She pulled on a soft cashmere sweater and a pair of jeans and padded over to the doors to the deck. Judging from the palm trees across the street where the herons' nest was, the wind had died down considerably. And it was a little bit warmer.

She glanced down at the deck and groaned. Slipping on her shoes, she headed out to the deck and grabbed a broom. The pile of shingles that had been blown off the roof was way too big when she finished sweeping, and it was clear that now storm season was upon them —which would bring plenty of wind and a fair amount of rain —she needed to get back to her list of repairs. She didn't really want to find out what would happen if it rained.

Faith rushed in the door with Daisy just as Jen poured herself a cup of coffee and reached into the refrigerator for the muffins she'd made the day before.

"Oh, Faith, thanks a million for letting me sleep in," Jen said as Faith shrugged off her sweater and hung Daisy's leash on the hook.

"No problem. It's not like Daisy gave me a choice, though."

Jen nodded. "It's true. Soon as the sun is up, so is she."

"Yep. Breathing right in my face."

"Oh, no. I'm sorry," Jen said. "I'll make sure to bring her in my room tonight and close the door."

Faith poured a cup of coffee. "I honestly had a nice time. We walked really fast, all the way to the pier. I could use the exercise if I'm going to see my skinny pants before Thanksgiving."

"Oh, good. Thanks for doing it." Jen gestured to a muffin, but Faith shook her head. "Nope. Refer to skinny pants comment."

Jen nodded in understanding. She couldn't count how many times she'd done the same thing. None of them were too obsessed with weight, but when your pants got tight, it was time for a course correction, no matter how brief. You could always try, anyway.

Jen filled up Daisy's food bowl while Faith was upstairs getting ready for work. Jen was thanked by Daisy's tail thudding against the kitchen island.

She slathered butter on a muffin and sat down, flipping through the mail. She separated out the important things from the unsolicited sales postcards from almost every business she could imagine. Realtors —she threw those in the trash —stores having sales —those went in the maybe pile —and several from local contractors. Those she kept.

With the wind last night and the shingles she'd found this morning, she was getting more and more nervous about the state of the house. Not much happened in the summer, weather-wise, and she'd been having so much fun that she'd been able to fix the urgent things and ignore the rest.

Now, though, the change of seasons and the weather wouldn't let her ignore it any longer. Joe had been nudging her lately anyway. In the evenings when they watched house remodel shows or house flipping shows, he'd remind her that she had a project of her own.

She'd always laughed, saying, "Why do you think I'm trying to get all these great ideas?"

There had never been any desire to ignore it, it just happened. But now she'd better get on with it.

She made a list of the contractors' names and decided

she'd call Dirk for recommendations. He'd been around Newport forever, and his job as a realtor probably had him come in contact with many local folks. Hopefully, he could help her steer clear of any bad ones and find a responsible, and hopefully inexpensive option.

Faith bounded down the stairs, all ready for work. She set her mug in the sink and grabbed her purse. "I ran into Joe on the walk today. Daisy and Boris had a chat, and so did Joe and I."

"Oh?" Jen responded, feeling the quick smile spread at the mention of Joe.

"Yep. And I have a bone to pick with you, ma'am."

Jen set down her coffee and raised her eyebrows. "Uh-oh."

Faith laughed. "Just kidding. Well, kind of."

Jen couldn't imagine what Joe could have said that would make Faith feel that way.

Purse in hand, Faith grabbed her keys and headed toward the door. "And don't think I'll forget about it by the time I get off work. I won't."

Jen frowned, but since Faith was smiling and gave her a wink, she wasn't too awful worried.

"Oh, come on. You can't leave it like that."

Faith started to close the door but stuck her head back in for a quick second. "Can't help it. I'm late. You'll have to wait to get information like I did. And turnabout's fair play."

With another laugh, she shut the door and was gone. Fair enough. Jen really should have told Faith and Carrie last night that she was seeing Joe so much, and how much she enjoyed getting to know him. But Jen had been worried about Faith and then—Faith had fallen asleep.

Jen decided she'd tell her friends tonight at dinner, but then remembered that she'd invited Joe. She'd just have to figure out a time before dinner to let them know. It wasn't really that big a deal —they just got together a fair amount, so nothing really to tell.

That's what she'd been telling herself, anyway, but she was starting to realize it wasn't true. There was something to tell, and it was a good something. And suddenly she was very excited to share it with her best friends.

Right after Faith left, Jen looked up at a knock on the door. She opened it to see a tall man with strawberry blond hair, a mustache and about a million freckles.

"Oh, yeah, sorry to bother you, ma'am. I know this might not be a welcome time to ask you a question. Is it a welcome time to ask you a question?"

Jen was a pretty good judge of character, and even though he was a little odd, she didn't get any bad vibes from him. Actually, he just made her smile.

"Sure," she said, stepping out onto the deck and trying to close the door before Daisy got out —but she didn't make it.

"Dogs. That's a dog. I love dogs," he said. He bent down

to pet Daisy, and Jen was amazed her tail didn't fly right off, she was wagging it so hard. Daisy seemed to be a good judge of character, too.

"What is it? A border collie? I love border collies. I had a friend once with a border collie, one blue eye, one brown eye. That was a smart dog. It could round up a guinea pig like nothing you've ever seen."

Jen laughed —she couldn't help herself. "A guinea pig?"

"Yes, ma'am, very important," the man said as he stood, his blue eyes shining. "Dogs. They're really something."

Jen blinked a couple of times before she could remember where they were in the conversation.

"Can I help you with something?" she asked.

"Oh, yeah, right. I don't want to bother you. I can come back another time if that would be better. Would another time be better or is this an okay time?"

If Jen had met anyone else like this, she might be worried. But this man seemed really sweet, eager and just —talked really fast. About strange things. But now she was curious what he wanted to say. She glanced over his shoulder, and he'd parked a truck with a lot of construction tools and a ladder in the back.

"This is a good time. What can I do for you?" she asked, really curious now.

He stood back another step, and when he reached his hand out to shake hers, he had to lean forward. "My name's Keith, ma'am. Keith Lewis."

"Nice to meet you, Keith Lewis," she answered, shaking his calloused hand. "I'm Jen Watson."

"Yeah, I know, I know. I mean I don't really know, but I believe you if you say it's true. I just wanted to tell you that I was up on a roof across the street doing some repairs and you have quite a few shingles that have lost their grip, so to speak."

He folded his arms over his worn t-shirt and began to stroke his chin, looking up over the awning.

"Oh, yes. I know. I was just getting ready to call around for some contractors. I don't know any down here. Do you?"

He held his hands up and looked down at the ground, taking another step back. If he stepped back any further, he'd run into the fence, and Jen was so curious about this guy that all she could do is smile.

"Yeah, yeah, I know it's hard to find a contractor. Especially in these parts. I've been working down here for forty years and even I'm hard to find. But I wasn't looking for work. Just wanted to let you know. I've worked on several houses on this street, so I know when something's different. And that's different. The shingles are supposed to stay on the roof. At least that's what the experts advise."

He said all this with such a straight face that Jen outright laughed.

"Nice to meet you, Miss Watson. Just wanted to let you

know. I'll be going now. I have some guinea pigs need rounding up."

He winked at her, his blue eyes twinkling, and as he drove away, she couldn't decide if he was nuts, or quirky, or both. But she really liked him. He hadn't left a card or anything, but at least he'd told her his name.

She went through the stack of postcards —none were from him, which didn't surprise her. He was definitely not the type to do marketing by mail.

But she'd already thought maybe he was the one she wanted to help her. He was definitely entertaining, and he seemed genuinely concerned about her roof —and her safety. She'd ask Dirk later tonight if he knew anything about him. And maybe it would be as easy as that.

NINE

It was always a flip of the coin that decided how Faith would get to work at the boutique. If she'd had more time, she would have walked but her outing with Daisy had made that impossible. There wasn't enough time.

So when she hopped in her car, she had to decide which route would be quicker. And she never could decide. Taking the ferry from the peninsula across the bay to Balboa Island was the shortest route as the crow flies. But it was really a risk because only a few cars could hop on one of the two rotating ferries at a time and if the line was long...well, it could take a long time.

The wind had died down and it was a pretty day, so she decided that she'd be better off avoiding that possibility. She headed up the peninsula and, judging by the steady stream of cars going in the opposite direction, she was pretty positive she'd made the right decision.

Parking opportunities were not in abundance anytime in Newport, but on a lovely weekend day in the fall, they were even less so.

By the time she found a place to park, it was a couple minutes after the store opened. She'd have to make a mad dash for it to be on time. At least, though, had added to her step count for the day.

When she rounded the corner onto the main drag and had passed several shops, she looked up to see a few people standing outside the door of the boutique. She wasn't overly concerned because Patti, the owner, seemed to have her own sense of time that was only loosely related to the rest of humanity's.

She smiled at the potential customers waiting outside and tried to think of something to say, but she really didn't know what was going on, so she just smiled. Again.

"I'm sure the owner will —"

Faith was interrupted at a familiar loud jingling. "I'm here, I'm here. Hello," Patti's voice rang from down the street.

Patti was definitely as unique as her store, her colorful skirt billowing in the breeze. Her silver bracelets —the source of the jingling —flashed in the sunlight. Her hair was even unique. It was long, and she'd cut bangs that were now silver, but the back part of her hair was still brown. It really was pretty and between that and her exotic manner of dress —beautiful skirt made of unusual fabric —she cut quite a figure.

It was one of the reasons people liked the store, Faith imagined. The smell of incense wafted out as soon as Patti turned the key in the lock, and after the customers entered, Faith walked into the store. She really did feel at ease there —the dark wood figurines and furniture were somehow comforting to Faith.

Faith frowned when she walked into the boutique. She'd worked all summer at the tiny, yet funky, store on Balboa Island and had never seen it like this before.

Half of the display cases and almost all of the shelves were empty. She'd been working on the weekends since she'd gone back to her teaching job a couple of months prior, and maybe it had just been happening incrementally and she hadn't noticed. But there was no mistaking it now. The shelves were almost bare.

Patti had left for a buying trip at the end of the summer and had seemed to have enough inventory for quite a while, but it was clear that was coming to an end.

So, all told, she enjoyed it. Patti was a little quirky, but Faith also thought she was interesting, loved the inventory in the store and got to make some money.

Once they found themselves with a lull in customer traffic, Patti called Faith over.

"Faith, good morning," Patti said, her voice a little

strained. Faith set her purse in the back storeroom and looked around there, too —seeing virtually empty shelves.

"Morning," Faith replied with a smile in an attempt to lighten the mood.

"Faith, we need to talk."

In Faith's experience, those words were rarely followed by anything good, so she sat on the stool by the register and braced herself for whatever would come. She really enjoyed working at the shop, and hoped she wasn't going to be fired. She'd carefully constructed her budget to include her income there, and would be sorry to see that go, too.

Patti was an interesting person, and Faith had enjoyed learning from her. She was a little on the exotic side, but Faith had come to know that she was a good business-woman, very aware of her niche market. The boutique had been a fixture on the main street of the island for decades. When Faith had covered for her over the summer to the best of her ability, it was obvious that Patti knew how to turn a profit. It certainly funded her buying trips. All in all, a good situation. And she had very, very good customers who showed their loyalty through repeat business.

"Faith, I need your help."

This sounded a little familiar to Faith, so her concern about getting fired ticked down a notch. Several times over the summer, Patti had gone on buying trips and asked Faith to cover, which she gladly did —because she could since she wasn't teaching summer school.

She began to prepare her response in her head when Patti continued.

"As you can see, our inventory is a little on the lean side, to say the least."

Faith nodded. "I had noticed. Especially this weekend."

"Yes. It usually goes like that. We seem to have a lot — until we don't. Usually I'm a little more ahead of the curve, but I haven't had anybody to cover since you went back to your school job."

Faith knew that she had hired someone at the time that Patti had hoped could turn into management material, but that hadn't worked out. She hadn't been on a buying trip for months. So Faith felt like she could imagine what was coming.

"So, Faith, is there any way —any way at all —that you could cover for me here? I really need to hunt down more inventory for us."

While Faith did enjoy working at the shop, she wasn't sure who the 'us' was that Patti was referring to. She was just an hourly employee who tried to help out when she could, and she didn't think she could handle much more than that. In fact, she knew she couldn't.

Faith sighed, wishing her answer could be different. "Patti, I really appreciate how much confidence you have in me, that I could even do it justice."

"You did well over the summer when I left for those quick trips. This would just be a little longer."

The desperation in her voice tugged at Faith's heart, but it really wasn't something she could even consider.

"I have a full time job. And one that takes up extra time afterward. Who would teach my class?"

Patti waved her hand as if batting at a fly. "I'm sure there are lots of kindergarten teachers around," she said, obviously unaware that there were, in fact, not. Especially in the middle of a school year.

"If I were retired, I would certainly help. But I'm not. I'm sorry, Patti, it's just a fact."

Patti squinted at Faith, then smiled. "I know. I'll raise your wages. How does five dollars an hour more sound?"

Faith didn't even have to do any calculation in her head to know that it was a ridiculous suggestion. For a good businesswoman, Patti was completely oblivious to the real world.

She smiled gently and said, "I appreciate your offer, but that won't come close to replacing my current income."

"Oh, fiddle," Patti said, and Faith did her best not to smile. It didn't feel like quite an opportune time.

"Well, how much do you make there?" Patti asked, reaching for her business ledger.

Faith told her, and Patti's eyebrows rose.

"Oh. Well, fiddle again."

Faith did smile this time. "Besides, I've made a commitment, signed a contract. I can't just abandon my class."

"Your loyalty is one of the things I like best about you, Faith, but I wish it were to me. Especially during an emergency like this," Patti said with a slight pout.

Emergency wasn't exactly how Faith would describe it, but she supposed to a business owner it would feel that way. She also knew how much the boutique made, and while she wasn't privy to any debt the store might have, the figure was pretty hefty. Patti could afford a full-time manager if she wanted one.

"I'm sorry, Patti. I do wish I could help."

Customers streamed through pretty regularly for the rest of the morning, and Faith was on her third cup of coffee before her stomach began to growl. She'd meant to grab some hard-boiled eggs to eat for lunch but had completely forgotten while she was teasing Jen.

Just when she was going to ask Patti if she could pop down the street and get a sandwich, the phone rang.

"Good morning," Faith said when she answered.

"Hello. Could you please tell Patti I'm ready to see her? This is Bob from the bank. I told her I'd call when her documents were ready."

"Of course. I'll tell her." Faith hung up the phone, mildly curious what the documents could be about. But she had so much going on in her own life, she decided she didn't have room for it in her brain.

"Patti, Bob at the bank is ready for you."

"Splendid," Patti said, her bracelets jingling when she clapped. "I shall return." She and her skirt swooshed out the door and just as it closed behind her, Faith's stomach growled again.

She usually kept at least a granola bar in her purse and she dug for one, to no avail. She'd even settle for a bag of potato chips at this moment, skinny jeans be darned.

Patti hadn't said how long she would be gone and Faith couldn't leave until she got back. She hated to do it, but she texted Jen.

HELP. I'm starving.

SHE GOT AN IMMEDIATE REPLY.

NO PROBLEM. Leftovers from the 40s coming right up. Mwahahahaha.

FAITH LAUGHED in spite of her wish that Jen would just bring the boiled eggs. She really wasn't too picky and would be happy just to stop her tummy from rumbling.

To take her mind off her stomach, she did a quick

round of the shop, asking customers if they needed any assistance. She tried not to do that too often as people seemed to find her if they had questions, but it would kill the time until the cavalry came with some food.

Jen pushed the bag toward Faith when her stomach growled again. "Right. Sounds like I'm just in time."

"You are, and thank you," Faith said, relieved when she opened the bag to see hard boiled eggs and pretzels rather than leftover appetizers.

Faith spent the busy day taking great care to dust and re-arrange the inventory they did have, from the bronze elephants to the wood carvings, and even the little boxes holding exotic stone jewelry. It was one of her favorite tasks, as she had always wanted to travel but her life didn't turn out that way. This was the closest she could get to seeing things from around the world.

At the end of the day, she fluffed the pillows made from colorful fabric, some with gold beads and some with crystal sequins. The pillows she made were better, she thought. Even Jen and Carrie thought so. But these were pretty, too.

As they prepared to close up for the night, Patti made one last try.

"Are you sure? I know you love it here."

Faith sadly shook her head. "I do love it here, but I'm not in any position to take on that responsibility. I hope you find someone perfect, and I'd love to continue to help in my small way."

"Oh, fiddle," Patti said one last time before she turned and walked down the street with a frustrated wave over her shoulder. "See you tomorrow."

TEN

The extra sunscreen had been a good idea. Carrie had on sunglasses, a hat, and a long sleeved shirt. It was a little bit cool, but the sun beating down in the convertible could give a wicked sunburn, anyway.

"I always wanted a convertible," Dirk said as they cruised down the 405 on their way to San Diego. Bethany and Dirk's daughter, Abby, were doing an exhibition at the camp and Dirk and Carrie had been invited to watch.

After Bethany had stayed with Carrie for that month when Bethany's dad went to Europe, they'd kept in contact. Bethany even spent weekends with Carrie when tennis allowed, and it had really brightened Carrie's life. They'd been apart for so long that she had closed her heart so much that she hadn't realized how much. With Bethany back in her life, it was as if things were finally normal again. And joyful.

And hanging out with Dirk was an extra bonus. The girls had become fast friends, so they were thrown together quite a bit at tennis tournaments and camps. Not that Carrie minded. At all.

She glanced quickly over at him in the passenger seat of the convertible. His sandy blond hair peeked out a bit from under his baseball cap and his aviator sunglasses reflected the cars ahead of them on the road. It really was a lovely day.

So with Bethany's return, Dirk's friendship and her dental practice going well, Carrie felt like most things in her life were pretty good. Good enough that the fact she hadn't seen nor spoken with her mother in weeks didn't bother her in the slightest. In fact, it was a bit of a relief.

Early on, she'd asked her mother if she wanted to get together with Bethany, maybe for dinner or something. Her mother had paused for a moment and said, "No, thank you." She hadn't even asked after Bethany at all, but with their history Carrie was only disappointed, not surprised. It was probably better this way.

"There's a spot right there. Somebody must have left," Dirk said, pointing to the front row of parking, closest to the tennis courts.

"Our lucky day," Carrie responded, zipping into the parking space.

She felt like a typical sports mom as she got out the backpack with cool drinks and some snacks for them, and

Dirk pulled out the padded seats they could attach to the bleachers. It might be a long day, and they wanted to be prepared.

They found a good spot, and Dirk got them all set up. It took a while, but they were able to get the girls' attention and wave, and they both received big smiles in return. Bethany came over and sat down for a minute, gratefully taking the cool juice box that Carrie handed her.

"Thanks! I needed that. Tired of water. Warm water at that."

Carrie brushed Bethany's hair from her sweaty face. "Looks like we were in the nick of time."

"I could say the same," a voice said from behind Carrie. She turned and stood, thrilled to see Maggy, Faith's daughter.

"Hey, Mags. What a nice surprise. I didn't know you were coming," Carrie said after she gave Maggy a hug.

Carrie re-introduced Dirk to Maggy, as he hadn't seen her since Labor Day.

"Nice to see you again," Dirk said with a nod. "I'd imagine you'd be pretty busy. Great of you to come."

Maggy said hello to Dirk and moved to hug Bethany, who held up her hands. "I'm all sweaty. Just won a match."

Maggy hugged her anyway. "So am I. Just finished volleyball."

"You're just a couple of athletes, I guess," Carrie said as Maggy set up a chair on the bleachers next to her and Dirk.

"So different than years ago when Maggy used to be your babysitter."

"I guess so," Maggy said. "I was as old as Bethany is now when I did that. Seems like a long time ago."

Carrie nodded. It definitely did seem like a long time ago. "What a treat to see you. I didn't know you were coming."

Maggy took the juice box Carrie held out, holding it up to her forehead for a minute. "I wasn't sure if I could. I never know how long volleyball's going to take. Bethany texted last night and asked, and I really wanted to come if I could. Man, this feels good. I haven't had a frozen juice box after a game in years. My mom used to bring them."

"Where do you think I learned from?" Carrie asked with a laugh. "Faith is a pro at this stuff."

Maggy poked the straw in the juice box and took a big sip. "She should be. She's had enough practice at my games. Years, actually."

"Your mom seems to be a pro at a lot of things. I don't know how she keeps all of her plates spinning, to tell you the truth," Dirk said. He'd spent time with Faith on the weekends as they'd watch her get further and further buried.

"I know. I'm actually a little worried about her, to be honest. I talk to her a lot, but she's always got something she has to get to. I can't imagine she can keep this up."

Carrie nodded. "She actually fell asleep on the couch

last night at Jen's, almost mid-sentence. We covered her up with a blanket and tucked her in. And then when I talked to Jen this morning, she'd already taken a walk and left for her job at the boutique. I don't know how she does it, either."

Maggy let out a big sigh. "I try to get her to retire, or at least slow down, but she won't even consider it, really. I don't know why."

Carrie knew why, but wasn't going to share that with Maggy. She knew for a fact that Maggy didn't know how her college had been paid for. Faith hadn't wanted to tell her that her father refused to contribute, that Faith had done it all on her own. And Carrie wasn't about to break that confidence.

"She loves her job —both of them," Carrie said instead. "We're just trying to be supportive, make sure she can keep her head afloat."

"Same. I actually sent her a bunch of —"

"Potato chips?" Carrie asked, handing one of the small bags Jen had sent her home with to Maggy.

Her hearty laugh made even Carrie smile. "Oh, gosh, there were so many. I'm glad she shared them. Probably not a good idea to eat them all herself."

Carrie told her that Faith had had to abandon her skinny jeans, and Maggy laughed again and smacked her forehead. "I should have thought about it. I just want her to be happy, and I thought it might cheer her up."

Carrie patted Maggy's knee. "It did cheer her up. And it cheered me up. And it cheered Jen up. That was very thoughtful of you."

"Thanks. I'm glad. I'm going to try to visit more, even maybe for Saturday night dinner with you guys? It's closer than driving all the way home, and maybe I could even spend the night every once in a while. I think it might be the only way I get to see her until she comes to her senses."

Carrie felt bad for Maggy —they were all pretty worried about Faith. "That would be awesome, sweetheart."

"Look after her for me in the meantime, will you? It's hard being so far away."

"I know. And of course we'll look after her. We all will."

ELEVEN

Faith's first mistake was thinking it was a good idea to try to rest for a little bit before dinner. She really wanted to talk to Jen about Joe and have a glass of wine, but her feet hurt from her long walk earlier and work at the boutique had worn her out.

"You sure you don't mind? I promise, just a twenty minute power nap," she'd said to Jen.

Jen shooed her upstairs and turned back to her dinner preparations. "I'll have a glass of wine waiting for you. Take your time."

And the next thing she knew, it was over an hour later. She sat bolt upright on her bed and saw the sun about to set, the sound of voices filtering upstairs.

She splashed water on her face and sighed into a towel, leaning against the bathroom counter. The mirror told her Jen was right —she did look tired. And she didn't want to.

But her budget ran through her head, and she took a deep breath and squared her shoulders. She slipped into a comfortable dress, feeling a little bit lighter out of her tight jeans.

She ran a brush through her hair and swiped some lipstick on, hoping it made her look a little more awake.

Joe's hearty laugh lifted her heart. He really was an incredibly kind, interesting man and as much as she wanted to tease Jen, she honestly was very happy for her if she had found someone that she could connect with like that. Especially after all she'd been through as such a young widow. She deserved it, and Faith approved a hundred percent.

"Hi, Faith. Long time, no see," Joe said when she got downstairs. He stood and gave her a hug, and Jen handed her a glass of wine.

"Yeah, that was a nice coincidence," she said as she sat in the chair by the window with her comfy pillows on it. "How was gondoliering today?"

He set his beer down on the table and leaned back, looping his arm over Jen's shoulders and kissing her forehead, and Faith noticed that it was completely natural, as if he'd done it a million times before.

Jen blushed and looked down at the floor. She looked up at Faith with a sheepish grin and Faith cocked an eyebrow at her. She shrugged, and then got up quickly and went into the kitchen.

It didn't matter in the slightest to Faith if they were an item. To the contrary, she needed to just tell Jen as soon as possible the she was thrilled for her.

"Hey, guys," Carrie said as she and Dirk walked in.

Dirk and Joe shook hands before Joe grabbed him a beer, and they fell into their usual conversation at the beginning of every gathering.

"Did you see that play at the end of the second quarter?"

Faith took the opportunity to grab Carrie by the hand and pull her into the kitchen.

"I saw that," Faith said. She couldn't help teasing, just a little.

"Saw what?" Carrie asked as she poured a glass of wine.

Faith raised her eyebrows at Jen. "Do you want to tell her or should I?"

Jen scrunched her eyes closed and pinched the bridge of her nose.

"I meant to tell you guys last night, but we got side-tracked."

Carrie looked utterly and completely confused. "Tell us what?"

"Joe just put his arm around Jen and kissed her. In front of me, even."

Carries eyes grew as big as saucers as she turned to Jen. "What?"

Jen looked like a kid caught with their hand in a candy

jar. "You heard her, and yes, he did. And if you must know, it wasn't the first time."

Faith laughed. "That was very obvious."

"Aw, Jen, that's awesome. So you're an item?" Carrie asked, giving Jen a hug. "He's a fantastic guy. Couldn't be happier for you."

"Same here," Faith said, taking her turn to hug Jen. "He's awesome. I was just teasing."

Carrie looked down and fiddled with the hem of her orange t-shirt. "Well, if we're not keeping secrets, I should tell you that Dirk and I may have done that, too."

"What?" Jen knocked her on the shoulder. "Why didn't you tell us?"

"It was only once. Nothing really to tell, but if he kissed me once, I imagine he will again. I really like him. He's easy to be around."

Faith smiled at her two friends. "He really is. You guys, I can't believe both of you are in relationships at the same time. Didn't see that coming."

"Whoa," Carrie said, holding her hands up. "I don't know that I'd call it a 'relationship' at this point. We're just enjoying each other's company, and we have the girls' tennis in common. I'm just going with it for now."

Jen nodded. "Same here. I don't think I'd call it a relationship, either. I just really, really like him."

"And that's how it all starts, ladies. I know it's been a long time for all of us, but I clearly recall that's how all the trouble starts," Faith said. She laughed and lifted her glass. "Here's to lots of trouble. Good trouble, for you both."

"What's going on in there," Joe asked as he and Dirk came around the kitchen island.

They all three exchanged quick glances. "Nothing. Just getting dinner. You guys can set the table real quick and this will all be ready in a minute."

Faith and Carrie helped Jen carry platters out to the table, and Jen took the opportunity to ask Dirk about that guy, Keith Lewis.

Dirk swiped at his mouth with a napkin and laughed. "Ah, you meant the famous Keith Lewis. Or infamous, I should say."

Jen wasn't sure if that was good or bad. "Uh-oh. That doesn't sound encouraging."

Dirk held up his hands and leaned back in his chair, shaking his head. "No, don't get me wrong. He really is famous. He's been around a long, long time. Quirky guy, and does great work."

"Oh, that's good to know. You've had clients use him?"

"I used to recommend him a ton, but I had a lot of clients who wouldn't work with him."

"No? Why?" Jen asked. She wanted to make sure she wasn't getting into a bad situation, and if other people didn't want to work with him, that was a bad sign.

"They all said the same thing. They met with him, liked the work he did but said they just didn't know how to speak 'Keith'. And didn't want to learn the language. If you talked to him for any length of time, I'm sure you know exactly what I mean."

Jen laughed, but the others looked confused. "I sure do. He said he had a friend with a border collie who herded guinea pigs. And that he had some guinea pigs of his own he needed to round up."

Dirk gave an exaggerated nod. "Exactly."

Joe frowned. "You're sure he's not just crazy? Jen really needs help."

"Nope, he's one of the best, honestly. Works mostly by himself, great prices and fantastic, creative ideas. You just have to make it through the discussion parts."

Jen leaned forward and nodded. "Well, he's the one I want to go with, then. I think he's funny. And it's just a roof. He seemed genuinely concerned. What could go wrong?"

"Famous last words," Carrie said as she stood and began to clear the plates from the table.

After they'd cleaned up, Carrie and Jen went out onto the porch to see the men off, and Faith headed up to the deck to wait for them. The wind had picked back up again, and the palm fronds swayed frantically in the breeze.

The next thing she knew, Jen was jiggling her knee. "Faith? Faith?"

Faith blinked a few times before she realized she must have fallen asleep again.

"I don't know about this, Faith. You're trying to do too much."

Faith had actually been thinking about it a lot lately. And she had to be back at the boutique the next day. There wasn't an inch of room in her world for any fun —or sleep. And it was getting hard to keep up.

"I hate to say this, but I think maybe you're right. I just really wanted to make some extra money. I mean, working at the boutique was fun in the summer. But I don't think I can keep up with it during the school year. I need some time to take a breath."

Carrie sat back in her chair. "I saw Maggy today, and she agrees with you. She's worried, too."

"Oh, you got to see her?" Faith said, her heart lifting. "How is she?"

Carrie took a sip of her wine. "She's great, as usual. She just misses you."

"I would have loved to see her," Faith said, her heart heavy.

"You could have gone with us if you weren't working two jobs. Come on, Faith, maybe you should quit."

Faith sighed. Maybe they were right. What good was it to make extra money, retire early, if she couldn't see anybody or do anything during the years it took to get there?

"I'll look at my budget again tonight and see what that would mean. I really am tired."

Jen laughed and shook her head. "We've noticed. You've only been here twenty-four hours and have fallen asleep more than once. That's no way to live."

Faith agreed. "I know. Thanks for looking out for me. I'll see if I can swing it. I guess some things are more important."

"I agree," Carrie said, and they lifted their glasses for the last time that night.

TWELVE

Faith wasn't in any shape to go over her budget the night before, so after she walked Daisy early, she sat down with her computer and pulled up the spreadsheet. She'd been so excited about the possibility of retiring early that she'd been willing to do just about anything —including working more than was probably a good idea.

But that morning, she'd barely been able to drag herself out of bed. Her feet ached as if she hadn't sat down in weeks —and except for sleeping, she pretty much hadn't. She'd noticed that she was feeling her age more and more, and couldn't remember when she'd woken up feeling refreshed and —well, great.

She flipped through the numbers on her spreadsheet, one she'd carefully laid out so that she could retire as soon as possible with enough pension to afford her house payment and live comfortably. For a time, her house hadn't had a dime of equity in it after the housing collapse a few years ago, and it wasn't until recently that she'd been back in the black —even if it was very little. Her extra income had been intended to make that as big a margin as she could before she retired, and maybe she could refinance for a lower monthly payment.

She had to be honest with herself. She was a little behind because she'd taken the summer off from teaching to help Jen with the house. It had been worth it, but it was a fact that her budget wasn't where she wanted it to be.

But Jen and Carrie —and even Maggy —were right. The current pace she was trying to keep was unsustainable, really. And it wouldn't make any sense if she was so stressed she got sick, Heaven forbid.

And the truth was, she really only had herself to rely on. She was thrilled for Carrie and Jen that they'd met men they cared about, but that wasn't the reality for Faith, and she knew it. Which meant she had an even bigger responsibility to keep herself healthy and solid, for own best interests, but especially for Maggy. Her daughter had suffered greatly during the divorce, and the least Faith could do was try to keep things on as even a keel as possible.

"I'm going to quit," Faith said when she walked downstairs.

Jen looked as surprised as Faith felt when she heard the words leave her lips.

"You are?" Jen asked, her expression frozen. "I'm so

happy to hear that. We can throw a huge retirement party. But can you do that in the middle of the year?"

Faith shook her head and realized she hadn't been quite clear.

"No. I wouldn't anyway, but you can't. I'm going to quit at the boutique."

Jen looked surprised —and disappointed. "Oh, darn. I thought you meant you'd figured out how to retire."

"No, I haven't. And it won't speed things up any by quitting at the boutique, but that would give Patti the opportunity to pay someone else who could really be a manager for her. She deserves that, and I really could use the time. To sleep."

"Aw, Faith, I know you really like it there. But I do think it's for the best."

"I do too," Faith said with a firm nod. "Best for everybody."

Jen looked at the clock and poured Faith's coffee in a to-go cup. She reached into the refrigerator and took out a bag and handed both items to Faith.

"You're going to be late if you don't go. Here's lunch for you."

Faith definitely should get going, and she hugged Jen. "Thanks. You're the best."

Jen smiled and raised her coffee mug in salute. "You're welcome. And good luck. Call if you need me."

Faith had planned to walk to the boutique but hadn't

left enough time to actually be able to do it, so on the short drive she ran several ways to tell Patti through her head. By the time she got to the boutique, she knew exactly what to say.

"Patti, I —"

"Oh, Faith, you're here. I'm so glad. I've been buzzing around waiting for you," Patti said, completely interrupting Faith's train of thought.

"Really, Patti, if you'll just let me finish —"

Patti completely ignored Faith, interrupting again. "I'm so excited. I've been up almost all night. Can I please go first?"

Faith didn't have the heart to say no. Whatever Patti was excited about, she seemed about to burst. Faith's resignation could wait a little while.

"Sure," Faith said with a sigh as she sat down on the stool by the cash register.

"Great. I really am excited. Yesterday I went to the bank to talk over my finances. I got the numbers I asked for, and spent all night looking over the books. I was wondering if you might reconsider my offer if I can pay you a little more."

Faith was completely caught off guard. This was the last thing she'd expected. But it didn't really change anything. She highly doubted that Patti intended to pay her a full teacher's salary —and besides, she had responsibilities in the classroom and had signed a contract. She couldn't just quit.

"Patti, I really appreciate it, but I don't see any way to do it. In fact, I was planning to quit today so that you could find somebody full time who can really help you."

Patti gasped and took a step back, aghast.

"That's simply out of the question. You are part of Patti's Parlor. You can't leave."

Faith rested her head in her hand, not at all sure what kind of solution they could come up with. But Patti's enthusiasm —and disappointment —were definitely hard to ignore. And she really did love the shop.

And Patti wasn't going to give up. "We can find a clerk to hire and train to work during the week. If you work weekends and take on the management paperwork, pricing and payroll maybe we could swing it. Please, just think about it. I haven't bought any tickets yet, but you can see I need to leave as soon as possible or we'll have an empty store."

Faith couldn't believe what came out of her mouth next. "Okay, I'll think about it."

Patti bounced on her toes and clapped, her silver bracelets jangling.

"Oh, thank you. I'm really grateful. And I can't think of anyone else I'd want to take care of my baby while I'm gone."

Faith got to work and the day flew by. She had so many

thoughts rolling through her head that she wasn't even sure what she did. Before she knew it, it was time to close up. And by that time, she sure needed to talk to Jen.

Faith walked slowly to her car, disappointed that she couldn't help, but already starting to think about what she would need for her kindergarten class the next week. It took some mental gymnastics to end her weekends at the beach and teach on Mondays, but she'd gotten in a routine after this long. While she'd love to stay, she knew it wasn't an option, so she might as well accept it.

THIRTEEN

"Um, that's exactly the opposite of what was supposed to happen," Jen said after Faith had filled her in.

"I know, right?" Faith knew she needed to pack and head home to get ready for school the following day, but she just wasn't quite ready.

"Stay for dinner. We can figure it out. Carrie and Mrs. Grover are coming, too."

"Okay," Faith said with a sigh. Jen poured her a glass of wine and steered her out on the deck, nudging her into a chair.

Faith filled her in briefly, and also let her know she'd told Patti she'd think about it.

"I don't blame you for that one. I don't think I would have known what to say, either."

Carrie waved up to them on the deck before she

knocked on Mrs. Grover's door. "We'll be right there. Save the good stories," she said.

Jen laughed. "Well, maybe they'll have some good advice."

Mrs. Grover handed the peach pie she'd made to Jen, who took a big whiff. "You make the best pies, Mrs. Grover."

The older lady blushed, appreciating the compliment. "Thank you, Jen. I appreciate that, coming from a chef as fine as you are yourself."

It was Jen's turn to blush. Faith thought they were both fantastic cooks, and was looking forward to dinner after her weird day.

"So, what's going on? You guys looked like you were deep in thought." Carrie and Mrs. Grover took their places on the deck, but Carrie looked up as the wind started up again.

"Things have gotten odd at the boutique. Faith tried to quit today and —well, it didn't quite work," Jen said, passing a plate of warm brie, crackers and artichoke dip.

Mrs. Grover reached for a cracker. Cherry tomatoes dotted the plate and she popped one in her mouth while Faith filled them in on what had happened.

"I was over there the other day, and I have to agree, there wasn't much on the shelves," Mrs. Grover said. "I love the smell of patchouli there, don't you?"

Faith laughed at the thought of Mrs. Grover liking patchouli. It wasn't a scent that everyone appreciated.

"You like it there?" Faith asked, her head cocked as she glanced at Mrs. Grover. As she'd been talking, her brain had also been at work on how she might be able to make this work.

"I do. I've been shopping a fair amount lately, and I like it a lot. I always find interesting things. The incense is a particular favorite. I have several incense burners at home, I'll have you know." Mrs. Grover nodded, like it was the most natural thing in the world.

Faith, Carrie and Jen exchanged smiles.

Carrie turned to the matter at hand. "So, if she pays you double what you make now, that would be great to put toward your retirement. But can you handle it? Physically? Those bags under your eyes imply otherwise. I say that with love, you know."

"Thanks a lot," Faith said with a laugh. But they all cared about her, and Faith knew it. It wasn't as if she'd hadn't had the same concerns herself.

"I've been rolling it over in my head. The money would be great. And with all the commotion, I think I forgot to mention to you guys that Amy asked if I was willing to have a student teacher. If she's as good as Amy says, it would lighten my load at school."

They all looked up as the wind buffeted the awning,

sending the blue-and-white striped fabric billowing wildly. Carrie's napkin blew off her lap before she could catch it. All four ladies reached for their glasses and plates and headed inside at the same time, without speaking a word. And Faith remembered to grab the peach pie.

Faith had a tough time shutting the door against the wind. "That came up fast."

"Sure did." Jen peered out the window. "Whew. If this wind keeps up that awning's going to rip again. I just got finished patching it and putting it back up. Not to mention if it's windy here, it's windy back at the house. I'd better check on Michael and Amber."

"No word from them?" Faith asked. They'd turned on the news periodically, and while a few fires had been reported, none were close to Jen's house. At least not last time they'd checked.

"I'm sure Michael would have called, but I'll check on them anyway after dinner." Jen set the roast chicken, surrounded with little red potatoes, onions and carrots on the table.

"That rosemary smells divine," Mrs. Grover said.

"Thank you for letting me pilfer some from your garden," Jen responded, gesturing for everybody to sit.

They spent a good portion of dinner weighing the pros and cons of Patti's offer to Faith. By the end of the evening, they still hadn't come up with the best option.

Faith sighed and set down her fork. "I told her I'd think

about it, so I don't have to respond right away. And of course I need to run it by Maggy before I do anything. She's been pretty worried, and I wouldn't want to spring that on her as a done deal."

"Smart of you," Carrie agreed. "When I saw her, she asked a lot of questions, asked that we'd look after you. I wouldn't want her to be mad at us, either."

Faith laughed. "Right, it's all about you."

They lifted their wine glasses and toasted.

Mrs. Grover cleared her throat, and all eyes turned toward her. She took a deep breath and looked at each one of them.

"Thank you all for being so nice to me. I really feel part of the group."

"Oh, you are, Mrs. Grover. I can't believe it took so long for us all to become friends. And by the way, I love your outfit."

Mrs. Grover looked startled, and glanced down at her capris. "Oh, thank you. I've been trying to step it up a little bit since the fashion show."

Carrie leaned back in her chair and smiled at Mrs. Grover. "And it shows. You look very chic."

"Thank you," Mrs. Grover replied, her cheeks pink. "But what I wanted to say was I'd be happy to help at the store, Faith. I do love it there, and if there's anything I can do, please let me know."

Faith had always known that her friends loved her and

wanted what was best for her. It was extra special to her that she had even one more to add to the list —Mrs. Grover.

FOURTEEN

The stack of roof shingles on the deck reminded Jen that she really did have an urgent mission. Enough had blown off that it could be a real problem, and with the windy season here and the rainy season coming, she knew she'd better get on it.

Joe had stopped by the day before and gotten up on the roof. He'd nailed down some of the shingles, but didn't have much encouraging to say when he'd climbed down.

"This is beyond my ability as an accountant, I'm afraid. Or, more accurately, your roof needs more work than I first thought."

Jen frowned. "Wrong answer."

"Yeah, I know," Joe said with a laugh. "Nobody wants to hear that. But honestly, I think this roof has already had more than one patch job. It's the original shingles that they don't really want you to use anymore. It really should be replaced."

So as Jen made coffee for her and Faith and waited for her friend to come downstairs, she made a mental note to work on finding that contractor first thing.

"I'll take you for an extra-long walk later, after Faith leaves," Jen had said to Daisy, with an extra dog treat for a bribe. If Faith was going to make it to work on time, she'd have to get a move on.

"Faith, I have coffee ready," Jen called to her friend upstairs.

"Thanks. I don't have time for anything else," Faith said as she patted Daisy's head quickly. "Sorry, girl. I'll take you next weekend."

"Got you covered." Jen handed Faith a bag. "Muffins and lunch."

"Bless you," Faith said, taking the bag and setting her suitcase on the porch.

"You look a little better today." Jen had hoped her friend would get a good night's sleep but wasn't sure, after their talk last night. Faith had a big decision to make, one that wasn't going to be easy.

"Thanks. I decided not to call Maggy or even think about this for a few days. I'll see how it goes in class with the new teacher, go over my budget again then see what Maggy thinks. I can talk to Patti next weekend when I come back. I should know what to do by then."

Jen nodded. "I'm sure you will."

Faith wiggled the bag in the air and sipped her coffee. "Thanks again. See you on Friday."

The house was quiet after Faith pulled the door closed behind her.

"Well, it's just you and me, Daisy," Jen said. "And I'm talking to a dog already."

She made good on her promise and took Daisy for a long walk. It was still really early, and she didn't expect to see Joe. When she passed his house, the lights were still off.

Back at her own house, she topped off her coffee and set about making her to-do list. At the top was try to find the contractor, Keith Lewis.

Dirk hadn't had any contact information for him, and suggested she try the internet. A pretty thorough search turned up nothing —no website for him, which really didn't surprise her one bit. He didn't seem like the type to even have a computer, let alone a website. She wouldn't be surprised if he only had a land-line, actually, not even a cell phone.

She leaned on the counter, her chin in her hand, and drummed her fingers on the counter. If Keith had been around as long as everyone said he had, maybe Mrs. Grover knew him. Or knew of him.

She grabbed another cup of coffee and headed next door, hoping it wasn't too early for her neighbor.

Tapping lightly on the door, she stepped back, ready to

leave if there was no answer. She definitely didn't want to wake her up.

Mrs. Grover threw the door open wide and stepped back, her smile wide.

"Good morning, my dear," she said, ushering Jen inside.

Jen held out one of Nana's muffins and sat on the wing-back chair that Mrs. Grover had patted.

"This is lovely. Can I make you some tea?"

Jen held up her coffee mug. "No, thanks. I brought my own."

Mrs. Grover nodded, fetched her tea from the kitchen and sat opposite Jen.

"What can I do for you this fine morning?"

"I have a bit of a dilemma and I was wondering if you might be able to help."

"Of course, my dear. Anything at all. You've come to the right place."

Jen laughed, sure that she probably had.

"I'm pretty sure that we're going to need a new roof on the house."

Mrs. Grover nodded gravely. "Based on the shingles I've found in my garden, I'd say probably sooner rather than later, too."

"I think you're right. Anyway, I started to hunt for a contractor and this strange man just stopped by and told me I needed a roof. Not exactly like you needed to be Sherlock Holmes to figure that out, as you mentioned, but he didn't seem to be hinting for work. He just said he wanted me to know and then he left. His name is Keith Lewis. And I've searched for him on the internet but can't find him."

Mrs. Grover smiled. "I don't know him myself, but I know of him. They've been working around the peninsula for a very long time. As long as I've been here. I think they had more work back before all of these people decided to build monstrosities. They specialized in smaller projects. And from what I know of them, you won't find them on the internet."

"No?" Jen asked. "Then how can I find them?"

Mrs. Grover held up a finger and went into the kitchen, returning with what Jen vaguely recognized as a phone book.

Mrs. Grover took her sleeve and wiped what could only be a layer of dust from the cover. "I guess I haven't used it in a while. Good to have, though, for those of us who are old school."

Jen had received several on the porch of the beach house but always threw them away. She remembered them from when she was a kid, but with the internet, she couldn't imagine who would still use them. Nobody even had land lines anymore and they didn't publish cell phone numbers.

"Ah, the good old yellow pages." Mrs. Grover flipped

through the various ads in the back part of the book and finally pointed, handing the book to Jen.

"Right there. Lewis and Son."

"Oh, that's what you meant by them. He has a son, then."

Mrs. Grover laughed and held her hand to her chest. "No, Jen, he *is* the son. He's been in this business with his father forever."

Jen raised her eyebrows. "Oh. He's —he's —" Jen wanted to say that Keith was on the older side himself so she couldn't imagine how old his father was. Was he still working? And did she want him on the roof? All kinds of questions flooded her mind.

"I think his father is semi-retired now. I believe I heard that from someone. Anyway, there you go. You can borrow the phone book, but please be sure to return it. You never know when you might need one."

Mrs. Grover poured herself a bit more tea. She stirred it and was quiet for a moment, watching the cream swirl before she slowly set her spoon on the saucer. Jen thought maybe her eyes were misting and she hoped she hadn't caused any trouble.

"Mrs. Grover, are you all right?"

Mrs. Grover glanced at the muffin that remained untouched on the coffee table.

"You know, your Nana used to bring me a muffin every

morning and we'd sit and watch the sun come up, listen to the birds, watch the waves. I really miss her."

She swiped at a tear, then held out her hand to Jen. Jen squeezed it, feeling a little misty herself.

"I miss her too. And this is a nice way to feel like she's with us. We should do this more often."

Mrs. Grover nodded and smiled. "I'd love that, Jen. I really would."

Jen tucked the phone book under her arm. "Thanks for the help, and I'll see you soon," she said.

Outside the door, she glanced at Nana's garden and back at Mrs. Grover's house. She was glad that Nana and Mrs. Grover had each other, and were as good friends as she was with Carrie and Faith.

She sighed at the thought of being without her best friends and knew it must be hard for Mrs. Grover. As she walked in the gate of Nana's house, she vowed to go see Mrs. Grover more often in the morning, and honor Nana's memory while making new ones.

FIFTEEN

Later, Jen knew before she even opened it that it was Keith who'd knocked. She could see his truck out front through the windows as she headed toward the door.

She'd finally tracked him down, and after several calls he finally returned hers.

"You sure you want to hire somebody who doesn't return your phone calls right away?" Joe had asked.

She'd explained to him that she didn't fully understand why, but yes, she did want to have him do the roof. When she first talked to him by phone, he'd given her a list of references and in doing her due diligence, she'd called a few. The people he'd given for references had laughed at the very beginning, before they'd explained that Keith and his father, when he helped, did outstanding work at very good prices, but you had to be willing to give in to some of their quirks.

But she already knew about that, so it didn't deter her. They'd agreed he'd come over and do measurements and return now, Friday, with an estimate.

When she opened the door, she was surprised to see not only Keith, but an older man standing there with him. His arms were folded over his chest, and he took a step back when Jen opened the door. In fact, they both did.

"Hey, yeah, I know it's early. Probably too early to put your thinking cap on, but here we are," Keith said.

"No, it's fine. We had an appointment, remember? I was ready for you. Would you like some coffee?"

Keith held up his hands, and so did his father. "No, we've had enough coffee already to flood an island. Shouldn't have any more, then we won't be hungry for lunch and that would be bad."

Jen nodded and stepped out onto the porch. The morning was crisp and lovely, and she gestured toward the outside table.

Neither man sat down. Keith paced, and the older man leaned against the railing. He looked almost exactly like Keith —or Keith looked exactly like him. But he was handsome, the same reddish-blonde hair with a little more gray around the temples. She guessed him to be closer to her dad's age but really couldn't tell. The freckles made them both look like little boys —endearing little boys. Especially when they smiled, which was often.

"Yeah, this is my dad. And I'm the son. Of Lewis and son. His name is Earl. Earl Lewis."

Jen stood again and extended her hand. Earl gave it a firm squeeze and a hardy shake, with a tip of a hat he wasn't wearing.

She grinned and sat back down again. "Very nice to meet you, sir."

"Pleasure to meet you, too, young lady. Has this boy been giving you any trouble? Because I can take him back home and make sure he's busy rounding up guinea pigs or something."

Jen wondered if this was going to be more challenging than she'd thought, but they were mostly going to be on the roof so she still wanted to go ahead.

"No, Keith is great. I'm excited to hear what you guys think about this roof."

They both sat down, and Keith unfolded what looked like a paper towel with a lot of lines and numbers on it.

"I was up the other night and couldn't sleep. I think I have a good idea about how to keep the costs low and while we can't replace with shingles because of fire hazards —"

"All the codes are different now. Why, back in the day —" Earl interrupted.

Keith interrupted him right back. "She doesn't want to hear about any back in the day stuff. It's today. Just today."

"Right," Earl said, nodding gravely.

Keith continued, and Jen knew enough about remodels

and new roofs to agree —he had definitely come up with something innovative and cost-effective. She was pretty sure her brother and her dad would be okay with it, but it was reasonable enough that she could probably swing it on her own if she had to.

"How's it going?" Joe said from the gate, with Boris in tow.

Jen introduced him to Keith and Earl, and Joe stayed and listened in. They decided to talk again on the following Monday, and hopefully start the project that week.

Jen waved to Keith and Earl as they climbed into the orange truck.

"Now that is an interesting team," Joe said finally after they'd driven away.

Jen shook her head and ran her hand through her hair.

"You don't know the half of it."

"You sure?" Joe asked, his eyebrows raised.

"Positive," Jen said. "I called references, I think they're funny and charming, and his drawing was spot on. He even had a good idea that I hadn't thought of that'll keep the costs down."

"That's great, then." Joe glanced up at the gathering clouds. "Just in time, too. We've been lucky that there's been no storm to go with the wind. Good they can get right on it so you don't end up with a waterfall in your bedroom."

"Oh, bite your tongue. Don't jinx me. Everything's

been going so well, I just need the weather to hold out for a little bit longer."

"Done. Sending good weather thoughts your way. Got any coffee?"

"Sure," Jen said with a laugh, heading into the kitchen as he opened the door for her. "Won't be as good as your mom's, but I have some."

"I beg to differ. I've become quite enamored with your coffee. There's something special about it."

Jen smiled as she poured him a cup, and was pleased she'd made so much progress and it was still early. It was looking as if it was going to be a good day. Just the way she liked it.

SIXTEEN

"Thank you for all your help. I don't know how I did it without you before. What a blessing."

Faith meant every single word of it. Cassandra had started in the classroom the previous Monday and it was like Faith's world changed in an instant. Cassandra was organized, creative, kind and patient with the kids —all the things Faith would have asked for if she'd had the chance.

She had thanked Amy in her head more times than she could count, so decided to stop by her office on the way out to thank her in person.

"I thought you'd feel that way," Amy said with a wide smile as she leaned back in her chair in the principal's office. "I knew she was a keeper right away. So I'll thank you, too, for taking her under your wing. She'll be even better when I can give her her own classroom in January. Learning from the best."

Faith's cheeks heated. She'd often thought that the new teachers were so much more energetic, had learned so much more than she had in school even though she knew that her sharing her experience was something that would be valuable for any young teacher coming into the profession.

"She'll be getting her own classroom in January?" Faith asked, realizing that meant she'd only have a few months with Cassandra.

Amy nodded and leaned forward on her desk, glancing at the big white board on her desk that listed teachers, classrooms and assignments.

"I hope I'll be able to. I kind of stepped out on a limb. It'll completely depend on whether or not someone decides to retire early."

Faith thanked her again and left her principal studying the board. She hoped that Cassandra would find a spot, but in the meantime, she was just grateful for the help.

In fact, she was so grateful that she'd decided to call Maggy and pitch the idea of taking on extra duties at the shop. She'd had an opportunity to rest this past week —even design and make some pillows, which she hadn't had time for in quite a long time. She felt refreshed, in control of her life. She'd gone over her budget several times, and the extra money would go a long way toward shaving off years she needed to work to make full retirement benefits, and she wanted to do it.

"Mom, I don't know. I really think you need to slow down, not speed up."

Faith was silent for a moment, not sure how she felt about that statement. Sure, she was technically retirement age but after this week, she felt, if not full of energy, at least competent. But she understood her daughter's concern and appreciated her for it.

"Sweetheart, I totally get it. I deserve that. I've been burning the candle at both ends for quite a while. But with the extra money from the shop and the help in the classroom, this feels like a really good thing to do.

Maggy sighed loudly enough that Faith could hear it over the phone, and Faith knew she needed to give it a little more of a push.

"I can try it for a little while and if it doesn't work out, I can think of a plan B."

"Mom, what plan B? Patti's leaving. Leaving the *country*."

"Patti and I talked about hiring someone else during the week, and I'll just make sure that person can cover on the weekends, even if I have to do the books and accounting."

"Mom, I —"

"I know you're just worried about me, and I appreciate it," Faith said, so certain that this was the right decision that she was willing to bring out the big guns.

"Even if it doesn't make total sense, I just feel it's the right thing to do. Like I'm supposed to. Meant to be."

This wasn't the first time she'd said something like this to Maggy. Her daughter had heard her talk about karma, and destiny and just knowing when something felt right for many, many years so it kind of took the oomph out of her argument.

"Unfair," Maggy said with a laugh. "You know I can't argue. Intuition, and all that."

Faith smiled and knew her daughter was right. Faith couldn't argue with it, and neither could Maggy.

"Good, then. It's settled. I'll tell Patti tomorrow and I'm sure she'll leave during soon. Meantime, I'll figure out how to get her covered during the week."

"I can come and help on the weekends, now that volleyball season is over. Just call if you need me, but maybe I'll plan to come up next weekend anyway."

Faith always felt better when she was going to see Maggy, and this time was no different.

"That'd be great, honey. Jen and Carrie will be happy to see you, and we can invite Bethany, too."

"Nice," Maggy said. "I'll plan on it. And Mom?"

"Yes, sweetheart?"

"Just promise me that if it's more than you thought it would be, that you're honest about it. We can figure out the rest of the stuff. It's not worth you getting too stressed —or worse."

Maggy had had an aunt on her father's side treated for breast cancer when she was around ten years old, and it had really frightened her. Faith knew that Maggy harbored fears that the same thing might happen to her mother, but Faith wasn't about to take any risks with her own health. Precisely why she'd decided to quit before all of the planets aligned and changed the game.

"I promise, honey. I really do."

Maggy let out a sigh of relief. "Thank you. I love you."

Faith's heart swelled. She was a lucky mom, and she knew it.

"I love you too, honey. See you next weekend."

There were lots of hoops Faith needed to jump through between now and then, but it was her intention to prove to Maggy that all was well, she could handle this and that it was going to be one of the best decisions she'd ever made.

SEVENTEEN

Carrie jumped up as a wooden shingle clanked on the deck right next to her. She picked it up and held it out to Faith.

"So you going ahead with the roof? At this rate, you won't have any of these left pretty soon."

"No kidding. With this wind we get at night, they're coming off like crazy. And yes, I did get ahold of that quirky contractor and he's coming on Monday to pick up a check for supplies. He can start next week."

Faith wrestled the cork out of the bottle of chardonnay Jen had put on ice earlier. "That's a good thing. Your dad and brother were okay with it? That has to be a pretty penny."

Jen nodded. She hadn't called them yet, but had thought about it all day. They'd let her stay in the house and not insisted on selling it, and asked that she'd just be in charge of any urgent renovations —and this was urgent.

She set the new shingle in the stack with the others. "I'm just going to go ahead. I'm positive it's a very good price compared to other contractors around here, and it'll protect their investment. When I put it to them that way, they won't object. And besides, they both have money."

Jen took the foil off the mini French onion soup bites she'd made for their Friday night happy hour and passed it around to her eager and appreciative friends.

"How do you come up with all this weird stuff?" Carrie asked. "Don't get me wrong —I love it. But some of this stuff I've never even heard of."

"I'm still going through Nana's things. This is from the fifties and apparently was very popular back then. I should make it for Mrs. Grover and Mrs. Russo. See if they'd remember."

"So culinary history through appetizers. That would be an interesting book," Faith said as she took a bite herself and nodded with approval. "This is really good."

Jen picked up one of the mini French onion soup cups and took a bite. It was warm and rich —definitely one of the better recipes she'd found in Nana's collection.

"Yeah, right. I wouldn't buy a book like that but I bet a lot of people who know how to boil water would. Well, I'd buy it if you wrote it." Carrie laughed while she helped herself to seconds.

"That isn't my intention, but it's kind of fun, isn't it? We get to try stuff that's different. And you guys can be my guinea pigs and tell me what's horrible."

"Ugh. Beets. No on the beets," Carrie said, taking a sip of wine as if to get the memory off her palate.

"Agreed. It took me forever to get the purple off my hands, anyway. Not worth it. Although I am sure there are plenty of silent beet lovers."

"My dad is one, but I don't care," Carrie added, again shaking her head. "My mother may be a lot of things, but at least she wasn't the kind who made me eat stuff I couldn't stand."

Jen nodded. "Yeah, same. I didn't do that to my kids. I did ask them to try things once —one bite —so that they'd know what they liked and what they didn't."

"Oh, my gosh, the first time I fed Maggy bananas, she smiled at me —she couldn't have been even a year old yet. Then proceeded to spit them back out. Still smiling. Never ate a banana again."

"See? Now she knows what she likes and what she doesn't. But how can you hate bananas?"

Faith shrugged. "In her DNA, I guess. I backed off on the weird stuff for a while."

"Bananas aren't weird. Heck, they're a staple for me," Carrie said. "Perfect. Portable. No cooking required."

"I didn't back off," Jen said. "By the time Michael was two and could tell me what he wanted for his birthday dinner, he asked for chicken curry. And extra spicy, too."

"Ha, I remember that," Faith said. "It was hilarious."

Carrie nodded. "I do, too. Man, that was a long time ago. And now he's going to have one of his own. Unbelievable."

"He's sure grown up into a nice man," Faith said. "How did it go last weekend with the house. The wind and the fires?"

Jen took a sip of wine and nodded. "Good. They said that there were more eucalyptus leaves on the ground than on the trees by the time it was over, but that what fires did break out weren't close."

"What a relief," Carrie said. "Glad we don't have to worry about that down here. Floods and winds are bad enough but being in fire territory —I'd probably never sleep."

Jen had been thinking about that a lot. The house she and her late husband had built by hand was definitely in a fire zone, and she worried constantly when the wind came up. It wouldn't take much for it to go up in flames, and with it vacant, she worried even more.

"I've been losing a little sleep to it, to be honest. Been rolling around ideas. I know Michael and Amber are cramped right now in that tiny apartment, and it's going to feel even smaller when the baby comes."

"Ah, I see where this is headed," Faith said. "Maybe they could stay in the house?"

"Or rent it or something? I don't know. I'm not sure if

it's the right thing to do to just let them stay there, even though they'd be helping. It's a little confusing. And Max was supposed to be there, but won't be back full time until after Thanksgiving."

"Hm. I'm not sure what I'd do. You have options, though, since you don't have a mortgage. I wouldn't be able to do that," Faith said.

"No, but your house helped you put Maggy through college. And get her MBA, too. Look at her now," Carrie added.

"True," Faith said.

"It is true, Faith. All of our situations are different. We just need to decide how to move forward," Jen said.

They asked more questions about the appetizers Jen had prepared, and let her know which were keepers and which they could pass on. And finally, Jen thought it was about time to find out from Faith what she'd decided. She'd talked to her several times during the week, but hadn't gotten a final answer.

"And speaking of moving forward, have you decided what to do about the boutique?"

Jen and Carrie both smiled when Faith took a deep breath, smiled at both of them and said, "I can't believe I'm going to say this, but I'm going to do it. And I can't wait."

EIGHTEEN

Faith thought Patti might cry when Faith told her the next day that she'd be willing to take over management of the store during her buying trip.

"Oh, Faith, I've been hoping against hope all week. I even put a help wanted sign in the door first thing Monday morning. You know, manifesting what I wanted to happen."

Faith did know —it was something that she tried to do, too. She just wasn't as skilled at it as Patti was, apparently.

Patti dropped a lined piece of paper on the glass counter at the register. "I made a list of everyone who's ever worked here and their phone numbers. I thought maybe we could start there. Never hurts to ask, does it? Whoever we hire is going to have to open up for us Wednesday through Friday, so it'll have to be someone we trust. I only gave you names of people I didn't have to fire."

Faith had intended to dust the shelves first thing and re-arrange what inventory they did have to make it appear there was more. Since she'd just told Patti she'd take over management duties, she supposed this was more fitting — but she didn't want to do it.

It was part of the job, though, so she just started dialing. It took all morning for her to get through the list of names, and she'd had to leave some messages. No one that she had actually reached was willing or interested. People were either happy in their jobs, had had babies or moved away. It wasn't very encouraging.

"Patti, no luck so far. I've left a few messages for people to call me back, but so far no takers."

"Darn it," Patti said. "We're going to run out of inventory soon. I ran to Mexico on Monday and Tuesday and bought what I could, but there really wasn't a lot of things that were appropriate. I need to go further across the border, and maybe to Thailand."

Faith thought that sounded marvelous, and she really did want Patti to be able to go. She began to open the boxes and price the items that Patti had been able to purchase, and set about arranging them on the shelves. It helped a little bit, but not much. And as Patti said, the new items were pretty standard —any tourist could pick them up on a day trip to across the border. They really did need some more upscale, unique items.

Customer traffic was slow but steady, and it was almost

time to close when Faith looked up and smiled at their newest customer.

"Mrs. Grover. How nice to see you," Faith said, giving the older lady a quick hug. "I'm surprised to see you here."

Mrs. Grover inhaled deeply and closed her eyes. "I told you the other night I love it here. I love the patchouli, and after I leave, my clothes still smell like it."

Faith laughed and wondered what other interesting things she didn't know about her. "Can I help you with anything?"

"No, I'm just browsing," Mrs. Grover said, and she headed over toward the incense display.

Faith grabbed her phone when it buzzed. She'd heard back from all but one of the prior employees she'd called, and she crossed her fingers that maybe this one —their last hope —would be the one.

After a few minutes, she clicked off the call and set her phone on the glass jewelry case. "Ugh," she said, dropping her head in her hands.

"What is it?" Patti asked, poking her head out of the back room.

"That was the last chance, Patti. Nobody on the list is willing to come back."

"Did you tell them it was only temporary? They could make some extra money," Patti said with a twinge of a whine in her voice.

"I did. I tried everything."

Patti tossed her ponytail back over her shoulder. "Oh, fiddle. That won't do at all. I have to leave." She gestured around the boutique, almost a look of panic on her face. "We're down to bare bones here. It's an emergency."

"Ahem," Faith heard behind her, and she turned around to see Mrs. Grover was still in the shop.

"Hi, Mrs. Grover," Faith said as she crumpled the list of names and threw it in the trash.

"I wasn't eavesdropping, but I couldn't help but overhear. You're looking for some help here in the shop?"

"I am," Patti said, no longer whining but clearly annoyed. "You'd think someone would be honored to work here. It's such a wonderful shop. I pay well, and it's only temporary. I'm not going to be gone forever."

"Sold," Mrs. Grover said, her eyes twinkling.

Faith blinked a few times, not sure she'd heard her correctly.

"Mrs. Grover, are you sure? Have you ever worked retail before?"

"Oh, hush, now, Faith. I'm sure this lovely lady —Mrs. Grover, you said?"

"Yes. Caroline Grover."

"I'm sure Mrs. Grover would be perfect for the job," Patti gushed. She turned and grabbed Mrs. Grover's hands and actually kissed her on the cheek. "Thank you, Mrs. Grover. You're a lifesaver. You and Faith here."

She flounced into the back room, humming a tune and

when the curtain fell behind her, Faith laughed and rushed over to Mrs. Grover.

"Are you sure?" she whispered. "You don't have to. She'll find someone."

Mrs. Grover squared her shoulders and looked quite determined. "She has found somebody. I've noticed how busy you girls are, and since Jen's Nana died —well, I've been a little bit adrift. And since it's temporary, it's perfect. And I get to work with you and smell like patchouli every day."

Faith took a step back and couldn't contain her laugh. "Well, I guess it's you and me, kid."

"Yep. We're a team."

"Yes, a team," Faith said. "Now let me show you around so you can see what you've gotten yourself into. There may be time for you to back out if you want to."

Patti threw aside the batik curtains and swooshed back into the store. "Well, my flight is booked for Monday morning, bright and early."

Mrs. Grover and Faith shared a quick smile. "Looks like we're stuck now," Mrs. Grover whispered, and Faith smiled. She could think of a million things that would be worse than this, and it actually sounded like fun.

NINETEEN

Mrs. Grover and Faith met early at the boutique the next day, and Faith showed her how to open up, work the cash register and do the other things that would need to be done on Wednesday, Thursday and Friday while Faith couldn't be there.

"And Jen could be here in a flash if you need anything. In fact, she offered to work with you, but I don't really think we need two people here on weekdays at this time of year. There aren't many tourists since school's in session. And if Patti's not back by Thanksgiving break, I can work with you."

Mrs. Grover fanned herself with a receipt book. "Oh, that makes me feel a little better. I wasn't nervous until the cash register part."

Faith knew what she meant. She'd been nervous, too,

in the beginning. But she'd gotten over it quickly and knew it would be the same for Mrs. Grover.

"Also, I'll take you next door, to the shops on both sides. They're small, too, and the owners are very nice. They could help if you need anything. I'll be sure to leave their cell phone numbers."

And when Faith and Mrs. Grover took a lunch break, she did just that.

After lunch, she let Mrs. Grover pretty much run the shop by herself —Patti had left right after they'd gotten back, saying she had to pack. Which she probably did, but she certainly wasn't letting any moss grow under her feet. Faith would probably feel the same way herself if she was lucky enough to be heading off to Morocco.

"Enjoy your purchase," Mrs. Grover said from behind the cash register.

"Check you out. You're a pro already," Faith said after Mrs. Grover smiled and handed a customer their purchase, which she'd neatly placed in tissue paper, a purple net bag with a satin ribbon and into a brown paper bag with handles.

"Well, thank you very much. It's been fun. And I really think I'll be fine here."

"I know you will, Mrs. Grover. And thank you so much for helping out. You're really a lifesaver."

It was almost time to close, and there was only one customer left in the boutique.

"Why don't you go add up the receipts for the day and I can take a look while I'm here. That's really the last thing to go over. I'll take this customer."

Mrs. Grover gave Faith a quick salute and headed to the cash register.

Faith walked up behind a tall man who held a beautiful necklace in his hand. She'd learned to say something before she got too close so as not to startle the customers after another clerk who'd been working there didn't, and a woman dropped a very, very expensive crystal figurine of an Indian goddess.

"That's a beautiful stone," she said, sincere in her assessment of the purple gem.

He was tall —she barely came to his shoulder —and when he turned, he smiled.

"It is, isn't it? I've only seen this stone one place before. It was in Chile, I think. Can't remember exactly. But they're not something you see frequently."

It was actually one of Faith's favorite pieces, and she remembered asking Patti where it was from when she'd unpacked it.

"Peru." Faith glanced again at the beautiful silver work.

"Ah, of course. I should have remembered. That's where I saw it. There were lots of them in the bazaar and I've kicked myself more than once that I didn't buy a few when I was there the last time."

"The last time?" Faith said, wondering who was lucky enough to go to Peru not only once, but more than once.

He turned again to glance at her and smiled. He looked a little embarrassed and studied his shoes for long enough that Faith wondered what he was doing. She looked down at his shoes, too, and there didn't seem to be anything wrong. Ordinary deck shoes, pretty common in Newport.

He finally chuckled and said, "Yeah. I guess I travel a lot."

"Lucky you," Faith said, quite sincerely. "I've always wanted to travel."

"You haven't? Why not?" he asked, with equal sincerity, as if he couldn't understand why she wouldn't.

"Long story," she said, not wanting to get into the details of why she wasn't able to use her one-way ticket to France when she was much, much younger and why it had never been possible afterward.

"Ah. We all have long stories, don't we? Some saved for other times." He smiled warmly at her again and handed her the necklace. "I'll take this if you don't mind."

Faith nodded and smiled, heading toward the cash register. Just as he was finished paying, Mrs. Grover came out from the back office.

The man put his wallet in his back pocket and took the necklace that Faith had slipped into a pretty purple silk bag with satin ribbon. He'd said it was a gift, and she wanted to make it extra nice.

"Thank you, and it was nice to chat with you. I hope you get to travel someday," he said before he turned to go.

"He seemed nice," Mrs. Grover said as she stepped up to the register and set the stack of receipts on the counter. "He was kind of cute. You should have invited him for dinner."

Faith cocked her head and looked after him out the store windows. "He was nice, but that's crazy. I don't even know his name. Bought a necklace, probably for his wife. We just chatted for a bit. He's traveled all over the world. And that's something I always wanted to do."

Mrs. Grover leaned her elbow on the glass counter. "That's funny. I never wanted to be anywhere but here. But why didn't you travel if you wanted to?"

Faith laughed. "It wasn't quite that simple. I had big plans that turned to dust. But everything turned out okay. I got Maggy."

"I'd say that's even better than a trip around the world, Faith. Although I've never had a baby or traveled around the world. Take it for what it's worth."

Faith chuckled, and knew she was going to enjoy working with Mrs. Grover. She was even more excited about it all now than when she'd come in earlier this morning and that was saying quite a lot.

TWENTY

It was all Jen could do not to hold her breath every time Keith —and his father —got up on the roof. Not for the first time, she wondered if it was all going to be all right.

The first step in the process was tearing off the old shingles, and the front garden was full of wood. Keith had painstakingly covered all of the rose bushes and other flowers with tarps, and Jen really appreciated it. But it was still a big mess out front, and she was glad Nana wasn't there to see it.

"Oh, my," Mrs. Grover had said as she walked by on her first day of work at the boutique. "I'm so glad your grandmother isn't here."

Jen laughed and nodded. "I was just thinking the same thing. I'm sure she would have rolled with it, but it's a little anxiety-producing."

Jen shielded her eyes from the sun and looked up at the

roof, where Keith and his father were engaged in their odd but entertaining banter.

"Everything okay up there?" she asked.

They both stood and tipped their hats to Jen —they were both wearing hats this time, against the sun.

"Yes, ma'am. All is well up here. What do you say, Cap'n?" Keith asked his father.

"All is well, mate."

They got back to work, but not before Earl gave Mrs. Grover an extra smile, and said, "Howdy, ma'am."

Mrs. Grover nodded, then turned to Jen. "You're very brave. I know they do good work, but at their age they could fall off any second."

"Don't think that hasn't crossed my mind," Jen said as she reached for a paper bag and handed it to Mrs. Grover.

"I thought you might like a muffin to take with you, to celebrate your first week of work."

"Oh, thank you. Today was the first day I didn't wake up with butterflies in my stomach. I hope everything's all right, and that Faith is pleased when she gets back."

Jen wrapped her arm around Mrs. Grover and gave her a reassuring squeeze. "I'm sure everything is perfect. And I'm right here if you need anything. Please don't hesitate to call if you do."

Mrs. Grover nodded and walked toward the ferry.

"By the way, I love your outfit," Jen called out after her,

smiling at the colorful, tie-died skirt that Mrs. Grover had somehow come up with.

"Thanks," she said with a wave. "I dug out some of my hippie attire. Thought it might be appropriate. Goes with patchouli."

Mrs. Grover consistently surprised Jen, and she closed her eyes for a moment, trying to envision Mrs. Grover as a hippie. She quickly realized she couldn't do it, and turned her attention back to the roof.

She'd called both her father and her brother, and they'd surprised her by quickly agreeing.

"That's a great price, Jen," her father had said. "Thanks for taking that on. That's exactly the kind of thing I wasn't interested in when I suggested selling. Remember, though, it's your and Greg's house now, so I don't really have a say. Make sure you call him."

Jen said she would, and she did right after she'd hung up with her father.

"Wow, great price," he'd said, and she'd finally let herself breathe a sigh of relief. She'd been prepared to take it on herself, but really didn't want to.

So, with all of the finances in order, she'd written Keith a check on Monday, and he'd started bright and early the next day.

"Wow. That's quite an operation," Joe said as he came up behind her.

"Understatement," Jen said, reaching for his hand and

pulling him up on the deck and out of the sun. "I try not to stare, but it's hard."

"I can imagine," he said as he took the cup of coffee she offered. "Did he say how long it would take?"

"Well, I've asked a couple of times, but the answers were long and convoluted, so I'm not exactly sure," she said with a smile.

"Still no regrets?"

She shook her head. "Nope, none. I mean regrets that I had to do it at all, but not with the selection of a contractor. He seems very thorough —he covered up all the bushes and cleans up every night. He even takes the tarps off the bushes and waters the plants by hand. I couldn't really ask for better. It's just —a big project."

"That it is," Joe said in agreement. "Well, I'm glad it's going well. And I hope it doesn't take too long. We've got high winds forecast again in a week or so."

Jen followed him to the gate after he'd finished his coffee. He kissed her on the cheek and she smiled as Keith said, "I didn't see that. Did you see that, Dad?"

"I didn't see that either. Nope."

Joe laughed and leaned forward, whispering in her ear. "You're sure?"

Jen kissed him once more. "Positive. Why don't you and your mom come for dinner tomorrow night? Tonight's happy hour, and —"

Joe held up his hands. "I know, no men."

"Well, it's not like that, it's just —"

Joe closed the gate behind him and smiled. "I know exactly what it is and I wouldn't dream of interrupting. I'll see if Ma's busy, but if she is I'd love to come anyway."

"Great. Any requests for dinner?"

"Hm. Haven't had pot roast in a while. And yours is the best."

"Pot roast it is," Jen said. "Perfect, as it's supposed to cool down quite a bit tomorrow."

Joe nodded and headed toward the gondolier dock.

Jen took another look back up on the roof and sighed. She needed to just go in the house. Maybe that would help her anxiety. And she could work on something for lunch for these two —they seemed to really appreciate it, and she loved to feed people who enjoyed it. These two characters wouldn't be any different. And maybe she could ask them how long it would take and get something resembling a straight answer.

TWENTY-ONE

Happy hour was fun, as usual. Carrie was in fine form, and they laughed until they cried when she described some of her foibles in her training class.

"I never in a gazillion years thought I'd be doing Botox injections. Holy cannoli," she said. "But my mom just wouldn't let up —and to be honest, I had dental clients ask all the time. All the other dentists do it, they'd say. And they were right. But man, it's crazy."

"Is it hard?"

Carrie laughed and shook her head. "No. Actually, I can hire a trained assistant to do it, but I have to be licensed myself. It's just —I don't know. Weird."

Mrs. Grover had stopped by, and Faith was happy to see that she'd survived her week. Faith had been quite worried, at least for the first day. They'd chatted that evening, though, and everything seemed fine.

Faith used the extra time she had and designed a few new pillows —brand new designs that she'd been anxious to get to. They'd turned out pretty well, and by the time she got to the beach house, she was rested, refreshed and ready to tackle the boutique.

She hopped out of bed the next morning and apologized to Daisy. "Maybe tomorrow, girl. I need to get to the boutique with Mrs. Grover," she said to the puppy as she grabbed a cup of coffee and headed next door.

Mrs. Grover filled Faith in with what had been happening during the week while they walked to the boutique, taking the ferry. It was a crisp, bright morning and the sun sparkled on the water. Faith loved the feeling of floating on the ferry, even for the very short ride, and by the time they got to the boutique, she was even more ready for the day.

"Boy, you weren't kidding about there being hardly anything to even sell," Faith said when she walked in the door of the boutique.

Mrs. Grover shrugged off her sweater and hung it in the back room.

"Won't take me long to dust, that's for sure," she said before she set about doing just that.

It took Faith less time than it normally would have to reconcile all the receipts for the week that Mrs. Grover had neatly separated by day for her. She'd never seen such a small pile in all the months she'd been working there.

Faith even opened the register and pulled out the cash drawer, hoping against hope that there might be more.

"I swear I collected them all," Mrs. Grover said, her hand on her hip.

"What?" Faith said, looking up. She blushed at the expression on Mrs. Grover's face. "Oh, I didn't —I never thought —"

Faith let out a breath when Mrs. Grover laughed. "I know you didn't. I was just trying to pull your leg. But it really wasn't slow —there just isn't much to buy. Not the unique things she usually has in here, anyway."

The shelves were pretty much empty, no doubt. Faith looked around the back store room for any extra boxes of inventory, but there weren't any.

She sat down on the stool behind the cash register and leaned on the counter. "I don't know all the details about Patti's business, but it hardly seems worth paying us to sit here and have nothing to sell."

Mrs. Grover shrugged. "I've lived here long enough to know not to guess about why rich people do anything at all."

Faith frowned. She'd been over Patti's books and, of course, worked with her for a long time now and Patti had never really struck her as rich. At least not her stereotypical version of rich. "What makes you think she's rich?"

"Well, the rent on this prime spot has to be astronomical, and the store has been here for years. And I do know that she sent both of her daughters to college."

Faith had sent her daughter to college, too, but she definitely wasn't rich. In fact, it had nearly bankrupted her.

"And if you think about it, stability on this street is everything. I don't think she'd want to close, even to save money. You need your regulars."

Faith thought about that for a minute. "I guess you're right. It's not high tourist season, but people do keep coming back to see if anything's new."

"Right. Consistency is almost more important than what you have on the shelves."

"I guess so," Faith said as she took one last look around the shop. "Several people did ask today when we'd be getting new stuff. I told them any day now."

Mrs. Grover laughed. "I said the same. But is that true?"

Faith shrugged. "I have no idea. Patti said she'd ship things as she found them, but that couldn't be faster than a few weeks, could it?"

Mrs. Grover pulled on her sweater. "Why don't you ask her? Then at least we'll know what to tell customers and they won't be mad at us."

"All right. I will." Faith didn't want to call as she had no idea what time zone Patti was in. She fired off a text and hoped that maybe she'd hear back by the following morning when they opened up again.

TWENTY-TWO

Jen finally retrieved the last bolt of fabric in from her car —
a task that would have taken much longer if Keith hadn't
decided to help.

It hadn't surprised her in the least, but she was grateful. She'd been feeding them lunch all week, and over the
course of their conversations she'd found out that Earl's
wife —Keith's mother —had passed away several years ago.

"Haven't had a sandwich this good in a long time," Earl
had said right off the bat.

"Nope. Nothing like this. My mom was a whiz in the
kitchen but these are something else," Keith had said. And
by the end of the week, they'd started calling her the sandwich queen.

So they were grateful —she understood that —but
they'd fallen into a nice rhythm and Jen actually appreciated the company. It had been a little lonely since Faith

went back to teach during the week. And they were definitely entertaining.

As they laid the last bolt of fabric down in one of the guest rooms, Keith said, "I know what I would be doing with this. I'd make a tent in the living room. Haven't done that in a long time. Maybe the guinea pigs would like that."

"Long time like fifty years," Earl added. "But you were really good at it. Turrets and everything. Never seen anything like that. He'd stay up all night and draw out what he wanted to do and then next thing I knew, it'd be done."

That hadn't surprised Jen, either. They both seemed to have an uncanny way of understanding how things worked, and should be put together. And she was grateful she was in good hands.

Earl tipped his hat and said, "Enough jawing, boy. Time to get back up there. Weather is supposed to turn and we can't leave this little lady with a skylight she didn't plan for."

"We could make her a tent in the bedroom," Keith said as they pulled the door closed behind them.

Jen looked around the room and wondered what she was going to do with all this fabric. She hadn't done much sewing all summer, and she was a bit envious of all the pillows Faith had made. So she'd decided to take a quick run to the house and grab some things —her sewing machine, some fabric and trim. Maybe she'd make some curtains, and try to spruce up her bedroom.

The house that she'd raised the kids in was so quiet that she'd actually shivered. Voices and laughter from long past rang in her ears, and she was sorry that it wasn't bustling with activity.

As she peeled potatoes and carrots for the pot roast as she'd done so many times in the past for her kids, she decided she needed to check in with her boys. It felt like it had been a long time since she'd had her whole family together. Thanksgiving wasn't too far away, and if she hoped to get them all in one place, she'd better start working on it now.

She'd check in with Max and see what his plans were —his internship should be ending soon. And also to check in with Michael and Amber, and see what was going on with them. Things seemed a little disconnected for her, and she wasn't used to that. It was just because she was living at the beach, but she wanted to make sure that her kids were all right, and that the house was too.

She spent the rest of the afternoon rearranging the guest room and nodded with satisfaction just before it was time to check on the pot roast. It smelled divine, and would be done right on time. She glanced at the clock and took the chilled bottle of wine out of the fridge as Faith would be arriving any moment.

Pulling on a sweater before she headed out to the deck, she arrived to see Keith and Earl packing up their truck.

"I think we've done all the damage we can for the day, ma'am," Keith said as he set his ladder on the side of the house. His father had rolled back the tarps and held the hose on Nana's rose bushes.

"Thank you," she said. "Can I offer you a beer or something?"

"No, no," Keith said as he ran his hand through his strawberry-blond hair. "That there's the devil's work. Right, Dad?"

Earl laughed and sprayed Keith's work boots with water. "Don't let him fool you, ma'am. Keith's been known to have a beer or some."

"Ah, Dad, you don't have to tell all my secrets. Like the time we were in Mexico and you —"

"Hush, son," Earl said as he handed the hose to Keith and hurried toward the gate.

Jen glanced over, and Faith and Mrs. Grover appeared. Earl stopped and caught Jen's eye, pointing to a flower and nodding, his eyes questioning.

"Of course," Jen said, a little perplexed. But she understood when he got to the gate, opened it wide for Faith and Mrs. Grover. He smiled at Mrs. Grover, tipped his cap and handed her a flower.

"A beauty for a beauty," he said.

Mrs. Grover turned fifty shades of red, and Jen and Faith stood, speechless.

"Aw, Dad," Keith said before he turned off the hose, grabbed his father and pulled him toward the truck. "See you tomorrow, ma'am. Don't mind my dad. He'll behave tomorrow, I promise."

The three of them stood in silence as Keith peeled away from the curb. His father leaned out the passenger window and waved his hat, his smile spreading from ear to ear.

"What was that all about?" Mrs. Grover said finally.

"I think it was pretty obvious, Mrs. Grover." Jen headed to the porch and poured them all a glass of wine.

"Beyond obvious," Faith added.

"Now that I think about it, I've noticed him looking your way when you walk by to work, and then on the way home. Looks like he's taken a shine to you."

Mrs. Grover looked down at her shoes. "Don't be ridiculous. I'm an old woman."

Faith sipped her wine and looked down the street. "Don't say that, Mrs. Grover. You never know when something good is going to come out of nowhere."

TWENTY-THREE

"Have you heard from Patti?" Mrs. Grover asked when she and Faith got to the shop. They hadn't had time to take the ferry, and Faith felt fortunate they'd found a parking spot close by.

"Nope. Not since I last checked. Guess we'll just muddle through until we do."

Mrs. Grover tended to customers while Faith worked on the previous day's receipts. Finally, just before lunchtime, Faith's phone dinged with a text from Patti.

I KNOW it's awkward but we can't close. I'm finding great things and have shipped some back already. Please just do anything you can to keep the boutique going. Thank you!

. . .

"WELL, I guess we have our marching orders," Faith said as she came out from the storage room.

Mrs. Grover waved goodbye to a customer. "And there went the last pillow, even. We've always had tons."

Faith looked over toward the corner where the pillows had been on display and sure enough, it was empty, too. Not a single one left.

"This is embarrassing," Faith said. "We have to have something to fill in with."

"Too bad we don't have any of your pillows," Mrs. Grover said.

Faith stared at her as if she'd said they should try out for the Dodgers. "Yeah, right. Mine aren't professional."

Mrs. Grover looked at Faith in equal disbelief, her hands on her hips. "You have no idea how great they are, do you?"

In her heart of hearts, Faith did think they were pretty, and certainly unique, but she'd never considered that other people might feel the same.

Faith frowned. "Not sure I believe you, but we really do need something to fill that corner."

"Maybe we could bring some in tomorrow."

Faith remembered that that she had all of her new pillows in the car. She glanced at the empty store and gritted her teeth, deciding it was better to have the shop full of something rather than nothing. She'd just have to get over it.

Faith squared her shoulders and said, "I'll be right back."

She headed out to her car and grabbed the trash bags full of the pillows she'd made. She probably should ask Patti first, but Patti wasn't the one who had to sit in an empty store and be embarrassed. If they put the pillows out, at least it wouldn't look so darn sad.

"What do you think?" she asked Mrs. Grover as she reached into the bags and pulled out several of her pillows.

"Oh, Faith, they're beautiful. You have no idea how unusual they are," Mrs. Grover said, running her hand over one of the velvet pillows Faith had made. No two were alike, and she'd worked particularly hard on that one.

"Thank you," she said finally. "Even if they're not as good as the ones Patti had, at least they're something."

"Don't say that. They're more than something. Better than the ones we had, even. And they'll fill that whole display quite nicely."

Mrs. Grover set about arranging the pillows, oohing and aahing over each one of them. "How did you make this one, with the cactus?" she asked, shaking her head.

Faith laughed. That was one she'd come up with after a trip to Arizona to see a college roommate. She really did enjoy the design part of it, and loved seeing her ideas come to fruition.

"Voila. What do you think?" Mrs. Grover said as she stood back and looked at the pillow corner.

"Looks silly to me, but it's better than nothing," Faith said. It was an interesting and unfamiliar feeling seeing them in public. But she knew there was no other option, and definitely better than an empty store.

Mrs. Grover sat on the stool, grabbed a pen and a stack of price tags. "How much do you want to charge for them?"

"Charge?" Faith said, a lump suddenly in her throat. Designing and making pillows had always been such a private hobby for her so this felt a little —well, a little vulnerable.

"You weren't going to give them away, were you?"

Faith wasn't quite sure what to say. It had been a little impulsive to bring them out, and she hadn't thought beyond that.

"I don't know. Five dollars?"

Mrs. Grover slapped her knee and laughed. "I don't think so."

She wrote on several price tags and placed them on the pillows. "There."

Faith followed her and leaned over, her eyebrows rising when she saw the price tag.

"That's —that's a lot."

Mrs. Grover nodded. "It's probably less than what it should be, but a good place to start. It's not even as much as the old pillows, and these are much, much nicer."

A bit of panic washed over Faith as she looked at the display. She was positive Patti wouldn't mind, but she had no experience at all with putting her designs —herself, really —out there for public viewing.

But it was good for the shop, and at least selling the pillows for what they cost her to make would recoup what she'd spent. Besides, it was Sunday and she wouldn't be back for a while. If the customers hated them, she wouldn't hear about it herself. Mrs. Grover would. At least until next weekend, anyway.

She still had a knot in her stomach when she dropped Mrs. Grover off after they'd closed the shop. Jen was waiting for her on the porch, but the lump still in her throat wouldn't allow her to tell her friend what they'd done at the boutique. Maybe she needed a little more time to get used to it —and to hear from Mrs. Grover after next week how it had gone.

Faith wasn't staying for dinner, anyway, so she gave Jen a quick hug goodbye, asked her to say hello to Joe and headed back inland to her real job. And her real world, trying to forget about all of her babies sitting in the shop where strangers could stare. She hoped they would be treated kindly next week, and she turned her attention to the work week ahead.

TWENTY-FOUR

Carrie couldn't remember her convertible ever getting so much use. And she also couldn't remember ever taking so much time off work.

Her assistant had rearranged Carrie's schedule more than once in the past couple of months with mercifully little eyebrow wiggling when she found out it was so that Carrie could go somewhere with Dirk. Andrea had supported Carrie in lots of crazy adventures over the years, and Carrie was grateful that Andrea didn't ask too many questions now that it involved a man.

And a very special man, at that. When they'd first met, and Carrie had introduced herself as Betty White, she'd never in a million years thought she'd become this interested in him. But through their experience with the fundraiser and tennis with her daughter, Bethany, and his daughter, Abby, they'd been thrown together quite a lot. And Carrie didn't mind one bit.

They'd taken the afternoon to drive down the coast to a smaller seaside village that was well known as a quirky artist's colony. Their summer art festival was world-renowned and Carrie had been many times with her mother—it brought people from all walks of life and back-grounds. Carrie and her mother always had front row seats to the annual pageant, and Carrie still tried to avoid looking at the charcoal drawing her mother had commis-sioned from one of the artists.

The crisp fall air hadn't turned cold yet, even though Thanksgiving was around the corner, but leaves were turning shades of red, yellow and orange even on the coast. As they drove down the increasingly rocky shoreline, the cliffs dropping sharply to the ocean, Carrie felt more peaceful than she had in—well, years.

Dirk was meeting with clients, but they were going to get a bite to eat afterward. Carrie spent the time waiting for him walking through the park on a cliff high above the breaking waves, taking a moment to sit and breathe deeply of the salty ocean air until her phone buzzed with a text.

WE'RE FINISHED. Come on over.

. . .

CARRIE HEADED TOWARD THE OLD, iconic restaurant where Dirk had been meeting with the owners. It wasn't a restaurant, exactly, but an older beach shack—hence the name, The Shack. It had stood in its current location for over fifty years, she knew, as she'd visited it frequently with her parents when she was a kid. Back then, it had been alone among restaurants on the beach, when the cliffs of the village were only dotted with small summer houses.

Back then, it had been a walk-up joint that served only grilled cheese sandwiches and hot dogs. The menu hadn't changed in all these years, but the restaurant had. She remembered being too small to even reach the order window, but now it had spread out a little bit, with some tables on a small patio, overlooking the spectacular view.

And the town had grown up around it. On the edge of the park, behind it was a pretty major thoroughfare, with the street dotted with artists' galleries, mini-marts and boutiques.

She slid onto the worn bench next to Dirk. "How'd it go?" she asked before he leaned over and greeted her with a kiss on the cheek.

"Well, I'm not so sure. The family is in a bit of a pickle. Not sure what to do."

Carrie frowned and glanced over at the The Shack—and the line that extended down the street. "What's the matter?"

"You know the family's had this forever. The newest generation has apparently gone different directions, and the older generation is ready to retire. Lots of commercial offers, but nobody's quite sure if they're ready to completely give up the legacy. Even with offers that involve lots of zeroes."

Carrie nodded. "What a difficult decision," she said. "Can you help?"

Dirk was an outstanding real estate agent, and had worked for many years in the area. "I'll do whatever I can, but at this point, it's more about them trying to get consensus within the family. And you know how hard it is to do that even in a small family. Theirs is huge."

Carrie laughed and knew exactly what he meant. "I'm an only child and my family can't agree on anything."

"Exactly," Dirk said. He smiled, and brushed some of Carrie's blonde hair from her face as the wind had picked up and she'd taken off her hat.

"Thank you," she said, enjoying his warm touch on her forehead.

"You're welcome. You know, you really do remind me of Betty White sometimes."

Carrie felt her cheeks heat at the memory of their first encounter. She'd tried avoiding him for months, and when it became no longer possible she hadn't wanted him to know who she was. Now, she was glad that she'd let him get to know her—more than just her name.

He leaned in and rested his lips on hers, and she forgot that they were in public, on a cliff, sitting in the fall sunshine.

He pulled away and ran his thumb over her cheek. He looked as if he wanted to say something, but didn't.

"Yes?" she prompted.

"I just wanted to say that I have really enjoyed spending time with you, and the girls. I hadn't realized that part of my life was a bit—empty."

Carrie nodded. "Same here. I had no idea what I was missing."

Dirk smiled and his eyes brightened. "I'm glad to hear that. And I don't exactly know what that means at our age. But I was wondering if maybe you'd agree that we're an item."

"An item?" she asked. "Do we really need to decide that?"

Dirk shrugged. "I don't know," he said with a laugh. I just wanted to say that that's how I feel about you, and was hoping you'd feel the same. So we could agree. At least that we're not seeing anybody else."

Carrie's eyebrows rose. She hadn't seen anybody "else" since she and Rob had divorced, so for her it was a moot point. She hadn't really thought about it, but she guessed they were.

"I think that's wonderful," she said. "In fact, I can't think of anything that would make me happier."

He smiled like a kid, and she thought she probably looked the same. He leaned in and kissed her, a bit longer this time.

TWENTY-FIVE

Carrie could hardly contain herself as she pulled up to Jen's for Friday night happy hour. She'd texted Jen that she was bring appetizers and knew the girls would be excited to see the gifts she'd brought from The Shack, and hoped that they'd be excited that she and Dirk were officially an item. She was pretty positive they'd be as excited as she was.

She bounded up the porch stairs and through the house, onto the upstairs porch where she could hear Faith and Jen laughing already.

"There she is," Jen said as she poured a glass of wine. "We've been dying to see what you brought for appetizers."

"Ta-da." Carrie set the foil packets on the platter Jen had ready and opened the foil. The sandwiches were still warm and gooey, and both Faith and Jen gasped.

"No. You went to The Shack?"

"The very one. Remember when we used to jack your brother's Volkswagen van and drive down the coast, just to get these?"

"Mmm." Jen nodded and clearly remembered.

"That was before my time, but I have been since. What a treat," Faith said as she bit into one. "It has been a long time. And they never change. Always the same."

Carrie's face clouded for a moment. "I figured we'd better get them while we can. Dirk went down to meet with the owners. Apparently, there's a big family rift and it might be sold."

"Oh, no," Jen said. "They've been there for —well, forever."

"I know. And the menu's been the same the entire time, since I was a little kid."

"That would be a real loss," Faith said as she helped herself to another perfect triangle of grilled cheese.

"And I have more news," Carrie said, her stomach fluttering. She wasn't quite sure how to say it, because it sounded so silly. So she decided just to spit it out. "I guess I'm Dirk's girlfriend."

Jen spit out her wine, and Faith stared at her and blinked a few times before she laughed.

"What?" Jen asked after she'd wiped up the wine.

"You know what I mean. I don't know exactly how to say it."

Faith patted her on the knee. "Did he give you the ring from a box of Cracker Jacks?"

"Okay, very funny," Carrie said, wondering how she could have ever thought they wouldn't tease her like this. "I just wanted to let my dearest friends know that we're — well, a 'thing'. That's all."

"Well, congratulations," Jen said. "We're very happy for you, although it's not a huge surprise."

Carrie gratefully accepted hugs from her friends, knowing they were, indeed, very happy for her.

Faith stood and bent over the railing, waving to Mrs. Grover as she walked by. "Come on up," she said.

"Speaking of 'things', Earl has been giving Mrs. Grover a flower every day on her way to work. It's really cute," Jen said. "She gets really flustered, but I think she likes it."

"Aw, that's sweet." Carrie stood and handed Mrs. Grover a glass of wine and scooted over on the upholstered bench. She marveled at how much the older lady had transformed since they'd first met months ago when she mostly stared at them out of her window next door.

"Hello, ladies," Mrs. Grover said as she took a seat beside Carrie. "Have I got news for you."

"You and Earl are a thing," Jen blurted out, then looked as if she hadn't meant to say it.

Mrs. Grover gasped, and said, "No, of course not. We haven't even stepped out together, nor has he asked me to. I don't move that fast, not like you ladies."

"Wait a minute —" Carrie started, until she saw that Mrs. Grover was teasing her, too.

"I'm just teasing. Honestly, I find him quite charming, and I certainly don't mind the flowers. But that's not what I was going to say." She turned to Faith with a big smile on her face, looking as if she might burst.

"Faith, the pillows are all gone. Every last one of them."

Carrie exchanged a quick glance with Jen. And Jen glanced into Faith's bedroom as if to verify that the pillows she'd designed were still on her bed. "What pillows are gone?" Jen finally asked.

Faith looked stunned, and Carrie wasn't sure at all what was happening.

"I —we —well, last weekend we were almost completely out of inventory. I asked Patti if we should just close down until she got back, and she said no. So I grabbed some bags of pillows I had just to fill the shelves."

"And they all sold out, like hotcakes," Mrs. Grover added, looking very pleased. She held out a piece of paper to Faith. "And look at this."

Faith's eyebrows rose and she turned white.

"Are you all right?" Jen asked, moving over to the deck chair next to Faith. She glanced down at the paper and her eyebrows rose, too. "Wow. That's nothing to sneeze at. That's good money for a fluke."

Faith looked like she'd seen a ghost still. "I —I don't know what to say."

"Wow, this is all very exciting," Carrie said. "Say you'll make some more."

"I can't, really. I have to go back to work on Monday, and I'll be at the boutique over the weekend."

Jen smiled and poked her thumb at the door to Faith's bedroom. "There are a lot of pillows on your bed. Tons downstairs and even some at Carrie's. We can at least bag those up."

"But —" Faith didn't look all that excited about giving up her own pillows, and Carrie reached for the paper.

She took a look and whistled. "No buts. This is great — a gift you can't ignore."

Faith still didn't look convinced, and Jen took the paper from Carrie, waving it under Faith's nose.

"Look, at least take in what you've already made, and we can come up with a plan. If they sell out again this weekend, you'll know what to do." She took another look at the number on the paper and nodded. "Faith, you have to. This could be your way to early retirement."

Faith shook her head slowly. "I can't even imagine that, but okay. I can take in what I've got. You know, they're just things that I've made for myself, really, and for my friends. I can't imagine anybody would want them."

Jen shook her head. "You don't see them the way other people do. They are unique, original designs. You couldn't find them in any store. Remember all the people who loved them during the open house? They're original and made with lots of love. Why wouldn't people want them?"

Faith's eyes misted, and Carrie knew Jen was right.

"Have faith, Faith," Carrie said, and Mrs. Grover giggled.

"Yes. You'll see tomorrow. People were clamoring to buy them, and I'm sure it will be the same."

Faith took the paper and tucked it in her pocket. "I'm sure it's just because there's nothing else in the store."

Carrie exchanged quick glances with Jen and Mrs. Grover. She was positive that wasn't the reason —she could feel it. And even if Faith didn't know it yet, this was truly a gift to her.

And it looked like it would have to be her dearest friends to convince her she deserved it.

TWENTY-SIX

Faith could barely go near the pillow section —actually the only section with any inventory in the store —without feeling nauseous. The weekend had been busy for that time of year, and every time a customer got close to the pillows, Faith turned toward the incense. She would have plugged her ears if she wouldn't have looked ridiculous.

Mrs. Grover, however, seemed to relish in describing the detail, craftsmanship and unique designs of the pillows. After listening to her for almost two days now, Faith had gotten a little less anxious. Not much, but a little.

They'd sold almost all the pillows by the time a woman came in near closing time on Sunday. She had an air about her that Faith had seen many, many times before in Newport —money, definitely, and a sense about her that she spent a fair amount of time traveling. Maybe even had more than one home, like many people in Newport.

"Hello," Faith said as the woman approached the cash register. "Can I help you with something?"

The woman's diamond earrings sparkled in the fading sunlight, and she set her very expensive designer purse on the counter.

"My dear friend, Mrs. Westland, said I just had to come in and see these pillows. We're looking for last minute things —my house is on the Thanksgiving home tour this year and there are just so many last-minute details. We've been searching for over a year for the perfect throw pillows for my living room sofa and haven't had any luck. She said I just have to see these, that they —"

She stopped mid-sentence and her eyes widened. She walked over toward the pillows and sighed. "She was right. This is exactly what I've been looking for."

She turned one of the pillows over, her hand stroking the beautiful, light green satin. She fingered the sea glass beads that dotted the corners and held it up to the window, shaking it.

It actually had been one of Faith's favorite designs, and one of the few that she'd made into a series. They were made from the same fabric with varying appliqués and different beads —some clear, several topaz, some sea glass.

Mrs. Grover had liked them particularly, too, and had said they'd go perfectly in her living room.

Faith had laughed earlier in the day when she noticed that the price on those particular pillows had mysteriously doubled —and she'd thought Mrs. Grover had done that just so nobody else would buy them. She figured it was a pretty safe bet at that silly price, and she intended to gift them to Mrs. Grover at some point.

The woman finally glanced at the price tag and gasped.

Faith stomach immediately knotted, but she reminded herself that Mrs. Grover wanted the pillows, and the price was ridiculous.

She almost fainted when the woman said, "And they're a bargain, too. I'll take all of them."

Mrs. Grover looked as shocked as Faith felt, and they rang up the sale in stunned silence.

"Thank you. They're going to put me over the top in the competition," the woman said as she flounced out the door and immediately pulled out her cell phone.

"Well, whaddya know?" Mrs. Grover asked as they watched the woman walk down the main street. She was clearly thrilled with her purchase and telling someone all about it.

"I —don't know. Not at all." Faith wasn't lying —she really couldn't wrap her head around what had just happened.

"Did you catch who she said had sent her in?" Mrs. Grover asked, one eyebrow raised.

"No, I didn't. Who?" Faith had been too shocked that

the woman even wanted to see the pillows to remember much of what she'd said.

"She said Mrs. Westland. Carrie's mom."

Faith turned toward Mrs. Grover, surprised. "Oh, it couldn't have been Carrie's mom. There have to be lots of Westlands around here."

Mrs. Grover laughed. "Nope. Just the one. And she runs the Thanksgiving home tour, you know."

Faith turned the sign hanging on the door from OPEN to CLOSED. She hadn't known that, actually, and couldn't imagine why Carrie's mom would send somebody in. She hadn't even seen Faith's pillows —had she?

There was only one way to find out, and she hoped Carrie would stop by for dinner tonight before Faith headed back to school for her last week before Thanksgiving break. And if she didn't, she'd make a point of calling her.

TWENTY-SEVEN

"Maybe," Carrie answered when Faith asked if she'd sent her mother in.

Faith shook her head. "You didn't have to do that. But thank you."

"You're welcome. I figured it couldn't hurt. She knows everybody in the entire world. Well, the world of Newport, anyway."

"So, I take it things went well." Jen set the lasagna she'd made on the table.

"That smells delicious," Faith said, her stomach reminding her that she'd been so nervous at the boutique that she hadn't eaten lunch.

"My first attempt at Mrs. Russo's recipe. We'll see," Jen said, setting down salad and garlic bread.

Faith filled them in over dinner, and they seemed

much more excited than she was herself. And not nearly as surprised.

"Of course, they are selling. They're gorgeous."

"Mm," Carrie said as she set her fork down on her empty plate. "That was really good."

Jen nodded. "Not bad for a first try. I don't want to give Joe any leftovers, though. I don't think it compares to his mom's."

"I think it's just as good," Faith said, patting her tummy which had thankfully stopped rumbling.

Jen shook her head. "No. Not enough white pepper, I don't think."

"Okay, so you tell me the pillows are 'gorgeous' and I'm supposed to believe you. Yet when I say the lasagna is just as good, you poo-poo me?" Faith asked, her arms crossed.

Jen opened her mouth to argue, then closed it. "Touché," she said finally.

Carrie took the last sip of her Chianti and set her glass down. "You're both right. The pillows are gorgeous, the lasagna was great."

Jen laughed as she stood to clear the table.

Faith hopped up for her regular job of putting away leftovers.

"Make sure to take some home with you for dinner this week," Jen said, and Faith happily obliged.

"So, what are you going to do now?" Carrie dried the dishes Jen handed her and set them on the island.

"Good question," Faith said as she got ready to leave. She'd packed her bags earlier and set them by the door, ready to head back inland for the week. "I think I have some more pillows at home in my work room, but I'll have to look. This is my last week at school before Thanksgiving, but I can't really make any more. It'll be really busy with the kids."

Carrie groaned. "I can't believe it's almost Thanksgiving. That came fast."

"Sure did," Jen added. "I've been busy watching this roof project, but I really could tear myself away, Faith. If I knew how to make your pillows, I would. I really don't need to watch them. It's mostly just been for entertainment, and they should be done this week anyway."

"That's okay. Thank you, though. Patti will be back soon, and this'll all be over soon."

Carrie's phone dinged with a texted. "Hm," Carrie said after she'd read the message. "I wouldn't be too sure about that."

"What do you mean?" Faith asked.

"It's from my mom. She said you need to have cards printed by next weekend for Mrs. Bradley to set on the end tables by your pillows. People will ask, and it's easier to have a card to hand them. With your business name on it."

"I —I don't have cards. Or even a business name," Faith stammered. "This is silly. Nobody's going to want one anyway."

Carrie set her hand gently on Faith's shoulder. "Faith, you're smarter than that. Look at all the pillows you sold just this week. Remember the numbers on the paper? That's real money. That's what you've always said you wanted. To retire."

"Right," Jen added gently, settling on the stool next to her friend. "This is what you've always said you wanted. Yeah, it seems like a fluke but it's certainly a divine gift so far. You can't stop now. Besides, you're always the one saying that you know what's right when you know it. And I think you know it this time, too. You're just scared."

Faith knew they were both right. She *was* scared. She'd always been happy teaching, helping her little kindergartners start their school path. But now she was faced with a fork in her own path, she wasn't at all sure which way to go.

"This was all getting to be too much for her, and her stomach was in knots again.

Jen stopped washing dishes and stared at Faith. Jen folded her arms over her chest and glanced at Carrie. "Well, you'd better get busy. A name and then cards."

"How about Faith's Perfect Pillows?" Carrie said, and Jen laughed.

"No, that's not fancy enough. Pillows for Posterity?"

Carrie shook her head. "Nah, I don't like that one."

"Hm. We're not very good at this," Jen said.

Faith groaned. "I can't think of a name, either. I don't

even know how you do that." Faith really didn't. She hadn't needed business cards as a teacher.

Jen snapped her fingers and grinned. "Too bad you don't know anybody who is a marketing professional," Carrie said, wiggling her eyebrows. "Knows all about branding. In fact, even helps companies do that very thing."

Faith sighed. "Yeah, that would be nice. I could use some help."

Jen rolled her eyes and Faith wondered why she was laughing so hard. "Faith. Did you forget about Maggy? Her MBA? A marketing professional?"

Faith closed her eyes. "Yeah, I guess I idd. I don't think of her that way. She's always just my little girl."

Jen wrapped her arm around Faith's shoulder. "She'll always be your little girl. But let her help you. Lord knows how much you've sacrificed to help her. Put her through school, even. She'd be honored to be able to help you for a change. I'm positive she would be."

TWENTY-EIGHT

It took at least five tries for Faith to actually will her fingers to call Maggy on the drive home. She'd start to dial, then hang up. She wasn't at all sure how to describe this silly turn of events.

Jen and Carrie seemed sure that Faith should play this out, but never in her wildest dreams had she believed that people might want to buy her pillows. There was no way she could wrap her head around the possibility that they might be her ticket to early retirement.

She finally screwed up the courage to call her daughter, though, having promised Jen and Carrie that she would.

"Hi, Mom. How was your weekend?" Maggy said when the call went through.

Everything came out in a rush, and Faith couldn't stop until she was done with the entire story —from Patti leaving to Faith's split-second decision to fill the shelves to the request for business cards. It all seemed so strange.

Maggy was silent for a moment, and then started laughing.

"What's so funny?" Faith asked, feeling a little defensive.

"You, that's what's so funny."

Faith frowned. "What do you mean?"

Maggy sighed. "What I mean is —my whole life you've told me that things happen for a reason. That we shouldn't over-think them, and we certainly had a responsibility to walk through open doors. At least that's what you said."

Faith nodded, even though Maggy couldn't see her. "And I meant it."

"Sounds like you meant it for everybody but yourself. Mom, if this isn't an open door, I don't know what is."

"Oh," Faith said softly. "I guess you're right."

Maggy laughed again. "Of course, I'm right. You're just scared. And I can help you if you'll let me. This is actually my job. What I do with the education you and Dad paid for. You might as well get a return on your investment."

Faith squirmed in the car seat. Her fingers tightened around the steering wheel, grateful for hands-free phones as she felt like she might cry, and she didn't need to get in an accident on top of everything else. "You know I never expected anything like that. I did that because I love you."

Maggy softened her voice. "I know, Mom. I was just

teasing. But can you imagine how good it would make me feel to help you for a change? It would be an honor."

That was exactly what Jen had said, and Faith felt her eyes well up. She sniffled as she wiped her cheek with the back of her hand.

"Are you crying?" Maggy asked, sounding alarmed.

"Maybe," Faith said, figuring if it was a good enough answer for Carrie, it was good enough for her. She tried never to cry around Maggy, not wanting to worry her. But these were a different kind of tears, and she couldn't help herself.

"Mom, listen to me. Big things like this are scary. They make us think about change, and opportunity. But like you've always told me, that's when we need to put on our big girl panties and meet the moment."

Faith laughed and reached for a tissue. "I know. I'm just scared."

"What are you afraid of? The pillows are awesome. People seem to like them."

Faith thought for a moment, wondering what she actually *was* afraid of. Over the weekend, she'd become a little bit more accustomed to people complimenting the pillows, so it wasn't that. And the money sure was nice, although she'd planned to give it to Patti.

It finally dawned on her, though, and she knew she needed to share it with her daughter.

"What if —what if it doesn't work? What if nobody likes them after all?"

Maggy paused on the line, and Faith could picture the face she made when she was thinking. "Ah, the old fear of failure thing."

"I guess that's it," Faith said slowly. She hadn't been in a position like this in years and years, and it was unfamiliar and —well, frightening.

"Well, a very wise woman has told me that you have nothing to fear but fear itself."

"I stole that from Franklin Roosevelt," Faith said with a laugh.

Maggy tried again. "Okay, how about no pain, no gain."

"Not original either."

"Okay, okay. Well, I know for a fact that it was you who encouraged me to try anything and everything that I was afraid to do, telling me that if I never tried, I'd never get to know how it might end."

Faith took in a deep breath, then sighed. "Okay, that one's mine."

"Yep. So, take your own advice. Let me help you play this out. You'll be so sorry if you don't."

And Faith knew she was right. She'd never forgive herself if she didn't even try.

"When did you get to be so wise?" she asked her daughter, picturing her deep brown eyes shining as they had since she was born.

"I learned from the best, Mom."

They agreed to talk over the week, and Maggy said she'd start with brainstorming business names. She explained they wouldn't need long to get the business cards and they could definitely be ready by the home tour if they decided on something Faith liked. Faith thanked Maggy for all her help, knowing full well she wouldn't be able to do this on her own.

"Okay! I'm on it. And Mom?"

"Yes?" Faith asked.

"I believe in you enough for both of us right now. Just put one foot in front of the other."

Faith held it together until after they ended the call, but her daughter's last words —words Faith herself had said to her daughter for almost thirty years —brought more tears, and she wasn't able to stop them.

TWENTY-NINE

The school week flew by—partly because it was the last week before a week-long break and partly because Faith and Maggy spent almost every night talking things over for the new business.

Maggy really was good at her job, and Faith was more impressed daily by the creative ideas she had. They'd decided on a name after hours of throwing things around, and when Maggy had emailed her the final layout for the business cards—including the beautiful logo she'd created—Faith teared up all over again.

They'd agreed that Maggy would come up to Newport Friday afternoon to bring the cards and stay for dinner, and the following day. Faith had to work, but Maggy had said she'd see if Bethany had a tennis tournament she could crash while she waited.

Everything was packed and ready to go for a proper

break, with only one last detail. Faith breathed a sigh of relief when Cassandra, her student teacher, said, "Do you mind if I take Jake home for break? I've become quite attached to the little guy."

"No problem," Faith had said, relieved she wouldn't have the hamster to worry about in addition to everything else.

She headed down to the beach house, the back of her car full of each and every pillow she could grab. She'd found a couple boxes full in the attic, and although she'd made them years ago, Maggy had encouraged her to go ahead and take them to the boutique when she'd texted Maggy pictures of them.

"Not too dated?" Faith had asked.

Maggy had asked for several pictures at different angles and lighting but had ultimately given her a thumbs-up for each and every one of them.

"What's the worst thing that could happen? Nobody buys them and they go back in the attic. This is really a no-risk decision," she'd said.

With that attitude, Faith had calmed down considerably during the week and was feeling much more peaceful. She felt like she could just be grateful, and watch things unfold.

"Fluff by Faith. How perfect," Jen said when they finally got to relax on the deck.

Carrie agreed. "I love it. It's great."

"Whew," Faith said, letting out a big breath. "We went through hundreds of names. Finally decided on that one. And Maggy's going to bring down the business cards tonight. Do you think one of you guys could run them over to the home tour house? I have to work all weekend."

"Of course," Jen said. "Keith and Earl should be finishing up this weekend, but I can scoot out early. Tour doesn't even start until noon, if I remember correctly."

"Thanks," Faith said. "I wish I could go."

Carrie leaned back in the deck chair. "Me, too. But we thought we should go spy for you, so we bought tickets anyway."

"Maybe that's for the best," Faith conceded. "I'd probably be way too nervous, wondering what people were going to say about my pillows."

Jen set out the evening's appetizers. "That might be tough for you. True. We'll report back, and you can just focus on selling more pillows at the shop."

"I promise I'll take pictures," Carrie said, holding up her phone.

"I want to go, too," Maggy said as she stepped onto the deck, her laptop and a box tucked under her arm.

"Maggy!" Jen cried, jumping up for a hug, and Carrie did the same.

"Hi, Mom," Maggy said, her smile wide. "How you doing?"

Their hug lasted a little longer than the others, and

Faith draped her daughter's hair back over her shoulder.

"I'm good, thanks to all of you."

"You're easy to love," Jen said as she offered Maggy a glass of wine.

"Long drive. Lots of traffic. Sorry I'm late," she said, gratefully taking the wineglass.

She took the top off of the box she'd brought in and handed Jen, Faith and Carrie each a business card.

"What do you think?"

"Wow," Carrie said as she looked at the card and ran her finger over the raised lettering.

"I second that," Jen agreed, holding it up to the fading sunlight.

Faith couldn't say anything at all. She just stared at the card with her name on it, a lump in her throat.

"What's this? Fluff by Faith dot com? And my email? Faith at Fluff By Faith dot com?"

Maggy looked like a cat who'd swallowed a canary. She opened in her laptop, typed something in quickly and turned it around so Jen, Faith and Carrie could see.

They each lowered their reading glasses from their heads and leaned forward.

"Oh. My. Gosh," Jen said first.

"Well, look at that, Faith. You're famous."

Faith glanced over the website with her name at the top, and a picture of her—one of the rare good ones—taken not too long before.

"Is that—is that ours?" she asked when she finally found her voice.

Maggy nodded, looking quite pleased with herself. "It sure is. I bought the domain name, created the website. And there's even a store for people to place orders. You just need to tell me the prices and I can put them in."

Faith clicked on the link that said 'shop' and took in a sharp breath. Maggy had used the pictures she'd sent to show off all of her pillows—even the old ones.

"We can change those out after you settle on which designs you actually want to showcase. But you have some of those now, so I thought I'd go ahead."

"Wow, smart cookie," Jen said. "You're really good at this."

"Thanks, Aunt Jen. I've learned a lot at this job and, of course, in school. And it was fun to do for somebody I really want to be successful."

"Yes," Carrie said, lifting her glass. They all toasted to Fluff By Faith and planned to do their spying at the home tour the following day

"Thanks, guys," Faith said, re-filling her wine glass. She realized that there was no backing out of this now—her friends and family weren't going to let her off the hook. But she was definitely relieved that the conversation turned to preparations for Thanksgiving the following week, and she almost—almost—was able to stop worrying for a while.

THIRTY

Faith and Mrs. Grover had just finished tagging and organizing the new set of pillows when the little bell on the door jingled.

"I love the smell of patchouli in the morning," Patti said.

Faith almost dropped the crystal figurine she was holding as she turned and saw Patti had returned.

"Oh, welcome back," Faith said, and she hugged Patti back when she wrapped her bracelet-laden arms around her.

"Thank you. Thank you very much. It feels like I just left," Patti said, taking a spin around the shop.

Faith thought it felt like she'd been gone for a year, with all that had happened but thought she probably shouldn't say that out loud.

"We're happy to see you. It's been interesting around here," Faith said.

Mrs. Grover nodded. "We ran out of most inventory a long time ago. We've been selling Faith's pillows, just to have something for customers to look at."

Patti cocked an eyebrow and swooshed toward the pillow section, her colorful skirt billowing behind her.

"Faith, I didn't know you made pillows." She picked one up and ran her hand over the cool satin. "How ingenious. And they're beautiful."

Faith was relieved that Patti thought it was a good idea, as there really hadn't been any other option.

"She even sold some to a customer who's using them in her living room on the home tour today," Mrs. Grover blurted out, much more interested in divulging information to Patti than Faith herself was.

"Oh, that's today? I always try to go, but I'm so happy to be back I just want to start unpacking. Wait until you see what I've brought back."

Mrs. Grover narrowed her eyes. "What I meant to say was Faith's very excited about her pillows being on display, and since you're back, maybe she could go meet her friends. See her pillows in the wild, so to speak. I can stay here and help you."

Patti looked up from one of the boxes she'd just opened and blinked a few times at Faith. "Oh, certainly. Yes, of course. Faith, we can catch up later."

Faith hadn't for one second thought she might be able to go, as she'd never leave Mrs. Grover alone on a weekend. This turn of events was a little disconcerting—she wasn't completely sure she wanted to go "see her pillows in the wild" as Mrs. Grover said. But since Mrs. Grover had stuck her neck out on Faith's behalf, she thought she should.

"Okay, thanks. I'll check in later, and fill you in about the books whenever you're ready."

Patti's nose was already back in the box, and she handed Mrs. Grover figurine after figuring. "Of course. No rush," she said.

Faith gave Mrs. Grover a quick hug and whispered, "Thank you," before she headed out the door.

Jen, Carrie and Maggy had already left for the tour, but Faith texted and asked what time they'd be at the house where her pillows were.

Jen said they'd meet her there at two, and said there was a map on the kitchen island.

GLAD YOU CAN COME! These houses are gorgeous!

THE BUTTERFLIES CAME alive in Faith's stomach, and she had second thoughts about going at all. But she remembered Maggy's words—one foot in front of the other —and decided she'd head out.

Faith wasn't very familiar with this area of Newport—
it was on the other side of the harbor, and high on a hill.
She got lost several times before she realized she'd kept
passing the house, as they were set far back from the
street.

She double-checked the address on the map and tried
to see past the tall pillars at each side of the gate, but she
couldn't. They each had statues of leaping dolphins, and
the driveway turned a corner right after that. She finally
saw Maggy standing out front, and sighed with relief.

Slipping her car into one of the few parking spots on
the street, she couldn't help but admire the spectacular
view of the harbor and the ocean beyond. She couldn't
imagine living in a house like that, and couldn't imagine
her pillows there, either.

Jen, Maggy and Carrie were waiting outside the gate,
and they all walked up the driveway together, admiring the
beautiful landscaping.

"I can't even imagine what a gardener here would cost,
let alone a mortgage," Faith whispered as they smiled and
nodded at people leaving the house.

"I know. You should have seen the last house. Oh, my
gosh. I have no idea what kinds of jobs these people have,"
Maggy said, her eyes wide.

They stood back while another group exited the foyer,
and then walked in. Faith's eyes adjusted to the change
from very bright outside to a little dim inside, and it took

her a moment to pick out her pillows in the living room as they entered.

"There they are, Mom," Maggy said, her voice filled with excitement.

They walked around the back of the couch, and Faith fought an urge to pick one of them up. They weren't really hers anymore, but it felt like they were.

"Look at those interesting pillows," a woman said to the friend she was with. "I've never seen anything quite like those."

"Fluff by Faith," her friend said after she'd reached for a card on the table that Jen had dropped off earlier that morning.

They both tucked a card into their purses, and Faith thought she was going to pass out.

"Did you hear that?" Jen whispered. "They loved them."

Faith let out a sigh, taking a quick look over her shoulder as she followed her friends through the remainder of the house. It was very unique, with floor to ceiling windows looking out over the bay, and onto a smaller, private garden in the back. Faith couldn't imagine living in a place like that, and it sort of felt like she was in a museum.

The had wandered through the entire house and were heading back through the living room toward the front door when Faith stopped in her tracks.

"Aren't those the most ridiculous things you've ever seen?" a woman with a large diamond sparkling at her throat said, pointing to Faith's pillows.

The three woman she was with laughed—actually laughed. Faith wanted to crawl in a hole when one of them said, "Looks like maybe she found them at Pillows R Us."

"*Fluff by Faith.* What a ridiculous name," one of the others said, and they all twittered as Faith's card fell back onto the table where the woman tossed it.

Jen, Carrie and Maggy all three turned to look at Faith at the same time, their faces white.

Faith was positive her face matched theirs, and she felt like her knees might buckle.

"Come on. Let's get out of here," Jen said, grabbing Jen's elbow and leading her directly back to her car, with Maggy and Carrie right behind them.

THIRTY-ONE

"I don't even want to look," Faith said when Maggy asked before they went to bed if she wanted to check for sales. "You can."

Faith knew she'd been a wet blanket all evening, but she couldn't help herself. Mrs. Grover had come over to ask how it went, and after re-telling the story, they'd all pretty much just fell silent.

They'd tried, though.

"Faith, those people just weren't your audience," Jen said.

"Exactly, Mom. Remember the first people who loved them?"

Carrie tried as well, in her own inimitable fashion. "They should be thrown off the pier in the dead of night."

Faith did chuckle at that one, but it didn't help for long.

But she didn't want to ruin everybody else's night, and she pitched in as much as she could when they made a shopping list for Thanksgiving later that week.

"I think I'll just do the traditional Thanksgiving, like we talked about last night," Jen said, mercifully taking the spotlight off of Faith—and her failure. At least she'd have something to focus on for the rest of the week, even if it was mostly cutting up onions and celery for the stuffing.

She slept fitfully, and woke up still feeling a little blue. Maggy had spent the night, and they both snuck out with Daisy to take a long walk on the beach.

"I'm proud of you, Mom," Maggy said when they reached the shoreline. "I really am."

Faith looped her arm through her daughter's, glad that she was proud but not at all sure she deserved it. "I have no idea why. It was a bust."

Maggy shook her head. "No, it wasn't. You put yourself out there. You were brave, and I admire you for even trying. And something else will come along, I'm sure of it. There are other things we can try. We can go to stores, see if we can place the pillows there."

Faith sighed and looked out toward the horizon as the waves crashed against the shore.

"No, honey. It's okay. I guess I'm proud we tried, too, but I've got to just get my head straight about teaching for a few more years. It's not like I don't know how."

"Aw, Mom. Don't give up."

"I'm fine with it. I've already decided. And I really appreciate you helping with all of this. You sure are talented. I'm very proud of you, too."

They walked back to the house in silence, and Faith quickly changed as Mrs. Grover would be arriving soon to head to the boutique.

"You leaving?" she asked Maggy before they left.

"No, I think I'll stay for the day. Maybe go see Bethany, take her out for a coffee. Then I can have dinner with you guys. I'll head back after that."

"That'd be nice, sweetheart. See you tonight."

Mrs. Grover stepped out of her house and bumped right into Earl, with a handful of flowers—a daily occurrence now.

Faith waited by the gate, but couldn't help overhearing their conversation.

"Mrs. Grover, today is our last day on the job next door. And I want you to know that getting to see you every day—and the cookies you've been bringing—have been the highlight of my professional life as a contractor. Er, my personal life, I mean."

Faith chuckled at the look on Mrs. Grover's face—she couldn't help it.

"And I was wondering if you might do me the honor of stepping out sometime. The thought of never seeing you again has me all wrapped up in knots like copper wire gone crazy."

Faith raised her eyebrows at the analogy, but Mrs. Grover seemed quite impressed.

"Why, Earl, I'd be delighted," she said as she took the flowers he held out, his hat over his heart.

"Yippee," he called up to Keith, who was on the roof trying not to watch. "She said yes."

"Way to go, Dad," Keith called down, with a whoop of his own.

Mrs. Grover now looked mortified, and she walked as fast as she could, grabbed Faith's arm and pulled her toward the ferry.

"I hope I didn't just make the biggest mistake of my life," she said under her breath. But she smiled and sniffed the flowers, so Faith was pretty sure she didn't mean it.

"You girls really did a bang-up job here," Patti said when they walked into the boutique. "I can't believe how many pillows you sold. It's just amazing."

She held out an envelope to Faith. "It's very generous of you to want to donate that to the shop, but they were your pillows. I left you high and dry. I kept ten percent just because I'd lose my 'good businesswoman' card if I didn't, but you need to take the rest."

Faith looked down at the envelope, and her eyes widened at the number scrawled on the front. That would go a long way toward her early retirement fund, even if it hadn't become the business of her dreams. It was better than she'd expected, and she decided that she'd settle for knowing she did her best.

THIRTY-TWO

Faith thought she was going to just rest and relax for the rest of the week, but she actually was glad she had something to do. After she got home from the boutique, Maggy had shown her that she'd had two pillow orders, and they were each one of her favorite designs.

She made both of the pillows on Monday, and then set about finding packaging, and deciding what was the prettiest way to wrap them. She went to the post office and got a postage scale, and Maggy walked Faith through printing the labels from her computer.

Faith and Jen had gone through the bolts of fabric Jen brought back, and they'd spent the evenings designing even more pillows.

"You know, this is fun. You can have a hobby now that actually makes money," Jen said.

And Faith agreed. She had learned a completely new

job, and it was fun, too. She got to be creative, and still make people happy with her pillows. And the money wasn't bad, either. Even though she wasn't selling much, every little bit helped.

She and Jen had gone shopping, and they got up early on Thanksgiving to stuff the turkey. They'd had Thanksgiving together for years now, and they got in a rhythm—Faith chopped, and Jen cooked. Carrie would be stopping by the store later on her way over—her specialty.

"How many are we?" Faith asked when it was time to think about getting out the dishes. They would be doing a buffet with this many people, but she wanted to be ready.

"Well, you, me, Carrie, Maggy, Bethany, Dirk and Abby, I'm pretty sure. And Amber and Michael."

"Okay," Faith said as she reached for the plates.

"Oh, and I invited Joe and Mrs. Russo. And Mrs. Grover. And Earl and Keith."

Faith laughed. "Earl and Keith?"

"Yeah. They said they weren't doing anything for Thanksgiving, that they usually just had Fudgsicles. I couldn't not invite them."

"Oh, okay. Good thing we got the biggest turkey in the store. I was wondering."

Jen looked a little sheepish. "You know how I always like to invite people. It makes me happy."

"I do know that about you," Faith said, and she gave

her friend a hug. "In fact, it's one of the things I love most about you, Jen."

"I love you, too, Faith. And I have to say again, I'm so very proud of you. You really put yourself out there. And you have a new income stream. You can probably quit at the store if you want."

Faith nodded. "Pretty sure I will. Patti doesn't need two people, and Mrs. Grover really likes working there. It's all perfect, really."

"It is," Jen agreed. "So much has happened since we came for summer vacation. Who ever would have thought?"

Faith shook her head. "Not me. That's for sure. And even though it hasn't all been how I'd hoped, it's all been perfect. I'm glad I tried."

Jen patted her friend's hand and nodded. She looked around the kitchen and smiled.

"Me, too."

"Am I too early?" Maggy asked as she came through the front door. "I probably should have called."

Faith kissed her cheek and took the pies and bottle of wine she held out.

"You're never too early. In fact, you can move right in, if you want," Jen said as she hugged Maggy, too. "Do you mind holding down the fort while we go change? The turkey's roasting, potatoes are peeled, and we can't make gravy until later. Other people are bringing everything else. Nothing to do but get dressed."

"Fine by me," Maggy said. "Don't blame me if there's any stuffing missing when you get back, though."

Faith laughed. "That always was your favorite. We're having a ton of people, so don't eat too much." Faith wagged her finger on the way upstairs. She hadn't been this happy in ages, and it felt good. Very good, and she said a little prayer of thanks, grateful for everything.

THIRTY-THREE

Jen and Faith each showered and dressed, meeting back in the kitchen.

"Perfect timing," Jen said as someone knocked on the door. "We've really got this down. And this year, we have a lot extra to be thankful for."

"Definitely worthy of celebration," Faith said.

They high-fived each other, and Faith headed into the kitchen to uncork a bottle of wine.

Jen opened the door and Mrs. Grover entered, followed by Joe and Mrs. Russo.

Jen took the warm dishes from her, and Mrs. Russo planted a kiss on Jen's cheek.

"Thank you for inviting us," she said as Joe helped his mother off with her coat.

"Of course," Jen said, setting the dish on a trivet. "Joe,

would you see what your mother wants to drink?" Jen said as she headed to the door with the next knock.

She gasped when she opened the door. Michael and Amber held out some flowers, and Jen couldn't get over how big Amber's tummy was getting. It was all she could do not to put her hand on her daughter-in-law's belly.

"You can, Mom," Michael said as he kissed his mother on the cheek.

Amber nodded, and Jen felt warm tears tumble as she gently rested her hand on her new grandbaby.

"Oh, my," Jen said softly. "Thank you. How are you feeling, sweetheart?"

"Good," Amber said with a vigorous nod. "Just trying to keep up with the baby kicking me all night."

"His father was like that, too," Jen said as she smiled up at Michael.

A voice sounded from behind Michael and Amber. "Did I kick you, too?"

Jen froze, hoping against hope that it was who she thought.

"Max?"

Michael and Amber stepped aside, their smiles wide.

"Oh, Max," Jen cried, tears spilling freely now while he grabbed her in a bear hug and lifted her off the ground.

"Hi, Mom. Been a long time," Jen's younger son said.

She stepped back and took a good, long look at him as he knelt to pat Daisy—his dog, actually, that he'd left when he'd gone to Boston. He looked older, somehow, certainly wiser. She couldn't wait to hear all about his internship.

"How long are you staying?"

"Until Wednesday, actually. I have a job interview on Monday."

Jen clapped at her good fortune and turned to look for Joe and Mrs. Russo. She introduced them, and Joe shook Max's hand.

"I haven't seen you since you were—oh, heck, maybe three? You're much taller now," Joe said as he looked up at Max.

"You were probably too young to remember, Max, but Joe was Dad's best friend. And does he have stories."

Jen smiled as they moved into the living room, and Joe and Michael showed Max the pictures they'd gotten out of storage of their father.

"What a lovely family," Mrs. Russo said as she looked around. "Thank you for inviting us."

"You're family, too, Mrs. Russo. It wouldn't be the same without you."

Mrs. Russo cocked an eyebrow and gave Jen a sly smile. "I was hoping you'd say that," she said as she lifted her glass of Chianti and set out to find Mrs. Grover.

Jen headed to the door with another knock. She opened it with a smile, and realized she'd completely forgotten to invite her father.

"Not like you to have a party without me, Jen," he said with a customary hint of a growl in his voice.

She reached out and hugged him. "I'm sorry, Dad. Come on in. And hello, Susanna," she said as he pulled his girlfriend through the door behind him, her blonde beehive almost hitting the top of the door.

She exchanged a glance with Faith, who mouthed, "oops," and reached for two more plates.

Fortunately, he spotted Max and headed into the living room, the slight forgotten.

"Not so fast, ma'am, not so fast. We come bearing Fudgsicles," Keith said as he climbed the porch steps, his father behind him. And sure enough, he held out a box of them.

"Couldn't possibly be Thanksgiving without Fudgsicles." Earl followed Keith in the door, scouting the room for Mrs. Grover. He handed Jen a bottle of wine also, leaning and whispering, "We're not complete heathens. Thanks for having us."

Carrie said, "Wait," as Faith began to close the door against the cooling afternoon. "I'm sorry we're late." Dirk was right behind her, and Bethany and Abby brought up the rear.

"Hi, Aunt Jen," Bethany said as she and Abby set two casserole dishes on the island. "My mom said she never brings anything, so Abby and I got some recipes online. I hope you don't mind."

"Not at all, thank you," Jen said and smiled at Carrie. "This is a first."

Carrie shrugged as Dirk took her coat and hung it on the rack by the door.

"I can't believe there are so many people here," Faith said. I think we might need to clean off the table outside. We can draw the curtains and it'll be warm enough. I saw some candles we can light, too."

"Good idea," Jen said as she met Joe in the kitchen.

"Whew," he said. "Quite a shindig."

Jen nodded. "Sure is. And looks like we have a lot to be thankful for."

"I know I do," he said as he turned her toward him and kissed her.

"Everybody will see," Jen said. "I haven't told the boys."

"They already know. And they gave me their permission to date you. It was all quite adult," he said with a laugh.

Jen's eyes widened and she laughed, too. "Oh, glad you all agreed who I could see."

"Don't do that. You know they just love you. And we all know Jen Watson only does what she wants to do."

"And don't you forget it," she said.

"This year, I'm thankful that I'm included in whatever that is," Joe said as he pulled his apron from his back pocket and got ready to carve the turkey.

THIRTY-FOUR

Faith, Carrie and Jen settled onto one of the couches as the men headed into the kitchen to do the dishes. Well, the younger set, anyway. Jen had trained her boys well, and Joe and Dirk were happy to lend a hand.

"Your dad seems to have hit it off with Earl and Keith," Carrie whispered when she leaned forward, trying to arrange pillows behind her back and not finding any.

"Weird, isn't it. I never would have guessed that," Jen said as she handed Carrie one of the old pillows that had been in the beach house for decades.

Carrie tried to punch it and put it behind her back, but she groaned. "I miss Faith's pillows."

Faith laughed. "I've designed a whole bunch of new ones and will be working on them even tomorrow. I've got lots of new ideas, and this couch will be the first place they go."

"Thanks," Jen said. "Hey, Faith, I'm sorry this didn't work out differently, but I'm still glad you did it."

Jen had said it already, so Faith was pretty sure they were feeling sorry for her.

"I know you are, guys, but I'm really okay. I'm glad I did it, too, and we've got a trickle of orders. It's fine. And it's fun."

"Good," Jen said.

Faith pointed to the window out onto the deck where the loveseat was. "Hey, check that out."

Jen and Carrie turned, and they both giggled. "Look at that. Maggy and Max. With their heads together. Dare we hope?"

Faith shrugged. "They haven't seen each other for a long time. Who knows? We can dream."

As they watched the two of them look at Maggy's computer, Maggy hopped up and showed something to Max. He gave her a thumbs-up, and they both came inside.

"Mom, can I see you for a minute? Outside?"

Max headed toward Jen and sat down in the seat Faith had just vacated. They had a lot of catching up to do, Faith knew, and she was really glad to see him.

"What is it, sweetheart?" Faith sat down on the loveseat beside Maggy and leaned back. The air was crisp, but it felt good after putting on such a big dinner. It was nice to get some fresh air.

"Um, I have to apologize. I haven't done a ton of website storefronts, and I may—well, I did do something wrong. I was showing Max the site, and he knew exactly what to change."

"He was born smart like that," Faith said. "I'm glad it's all fixed now. Nice of him to come."

"Yes, yes, it's nice to see him," Maggy said. "But I want to show you something. What he fixed is the order counter. Somehow, I had them re-directed to the wrong place. He fixed it. Take a look."

Faith reached for her glasses on her head, but she must have left them in the kitchen. She leaned forward and squinted, but she wasn't at all sure what Maggy was wanting her to see.

"Can you just tell me? I don't have my glasses."

"Mom," Maggy said with a twinge of irritation in her voice that reminded Faith of when she was a teenager.

"What?"

"The number of orders, that was five. It should have been fifty."

"What do you mean?" Faith asked slowly.

"It means you have a hundred and fifty orders," Maggy said, barely able to contain her excitement. "That's a lot of money, in just five days."

Faith blinked and stared at the screen. "I—are you sure?"

"Yes, I'm sure."

Faith leaned back in the love seat and rubbed her forehead. "I don't have fifty pillows. What am I going to do?"

Maggy patted her mother's knee. "Don't worry. When I set this up, I put in a four to six-week delivery time. And if I need to, I can put on there that something is back-ordered."

"Oh, my gosh," Faith said, and she jumped when Maggy's computer made a little ding. "What's that?"

"I've set it up so that every time someone orders, it makes the sound. To inspire you. I'll put it on your computer, too, first thing tomorrow."

Faith's smile began to spread as what she'd just heard sunk in. "I can't believe it. This is perfect."

"For now," Maggy said. "But if you've gotten this many orders in four days, we'd better figure out how to scale up. You personally aren't going to be able to make all those pillows, especially with your job, and when the orders come even faster—"

"Sshhh," Faith said, and she reached for her daughter's hand. She sat for a moment and looked at the stars, the waves crashing against the beach.

"I just want to take a moment to be thankful. To thank you, and to appreciate that we did this together. We can worry about scaling tomorrow, whatever that is."

Maggy laughed and rested her head on her mother's shoulder. "Okay, Mom. But you did it. You started a business."

Faith nodded. "We did it, sweetheart. We did it together. I would never have had the courage without you."

Maggy sighed. "And I wouldn't have had any courage without you either, Mom. Thank you. For everything."

Faith's heart was full, and she glanced one more time at the stars twinkling brightly in the night sky.

"You're welcome, sweetheart. We're quite the team," she said, and she meant every word of it.

EPILOGUE

"I think I had a turkey hangover," Faith said when she, Faith and Carrie met for happy hour the next night. "I slept like a baby, for the first time in a long time."

"You look great," Jen said as she cocked her head and took a better look at Faith—with glasses. "No bags under your eyes. I mean, not that you *had* bags under your eyes, of course."

Faith laughed when Carrie nodded so hard that she almost dropped her plate.

Faith knew exactly why she had slept like a rock, though, and she was anxious to tell her friends. There hadn't been a single second until now—people had come and gone all day, and Maggy and Max had both filled guest rooms overnight. Max had headed back inland to check on the house and had taken Daisy with him, so even Jen had had a good night's sleep, Faith knew.

So now, Jen had brought up a plate of leftover appetizers from Thanksgiving the day before, and they all just sat and enjoyed the cool evening breeze. The waves were pounding the sand pretty hard, and in another week it should be high tide.

But the peace and gratitude Faith had felt the night before at the realization that people were actually buying her pillows had given way to the realization that there was no way in her current situation that she could ever—ever—make that many pillows by herself. Even with a four- to six-week window. She had a job. She'd actually be going back to school on Monday.

Even when Maggy had whispered, "Don't worry. We'll think of something," it hadn't made her feel better. She'd turned it over in her mind all day long and still hadn't come up with a plan.

"You what?" Jen asked when Faith finally told them what had happened, that she'd gotten so many pillow orders.

"What the heck?" Carrie said as she tried to wrap her head around all of this, too.

"Yep. I can hardly believe it myself," Faith said. "And I was excited, I really was. And I think that's why I slept like a baby."

"What do you mean *was*?" Carrie asked. "This is what you wanted. It's a miracle. Well, not exactly a miracle, you deserve it, but you know what I mean."

Faith laughed. "I do know what you mean. But I've been thinking about it all day. There's no way I can produce that on my own. None."

"Oh, I brought all my sewing stuff down, remember? I can help. You just need to show me the designs and I can make them."

Faith shook her head slowly. "I appreciate you so, so much. And thank you. But you can't do it either. It's too much for even the two of us."

"I don't know how to thread a needle, or I'd help, too," Carrie said.

"I know you would." Faith knew deep in her bones that her friends would do anything they could to help, but she really didn't see a way to pull this off."

Carrie squinted at Faith. "If you didn't have a job, could you do it? You and Faith? For now, with this level of orders?"

Faith thought it over. "I suppose so. The hardest part is the design. That's already done. We're just doing production. So yes, I think maybe we could."

Carrie smiled, and she was practically bouncing out of her deck chair. "That's a lot of money, between what you made at the boutique and these orders. Surely it would replace your salary."

Faith wasn't quite sure what she was getting at. "Well, for now, but I don't know if it's going to continue. That's too big a risk. I can't quit my job now, based on just what's happened over the last few weeks. That's too scary for me."

"I know, I know," Carrie said, gesturing for Faith to hear her out. "What if, though, you asked Cassandra if she could take over the class just until the end of the semester? You could take a leave of absence, and see how things go."

Jen leaned forward. "That's a pretty safe bet, Faith. If it goes great, maybe you could retire early. If it doesn't, you still keep your job. What could go wrong?"

Faith wasn't used to making these kinds of decisions. She hadn't taken a risk like this ever—even though she'd wanted to long ago when she was moving to France.

But they were right—if Cassandra was willing and interested, it really would be the perfect way for her to try this out with as little risk as possible.

She didn't even need to talk to Maggy to know that in her gut, she knew it was worth a try. Open door, and all that. Who was she to thumb her nose at such an opportunity.

"Okay, I'll do it. I'll ask her and Amy first thing in the morning."

Jen's looked at Faith, astonished. "Wow, I didn't expect that. I thought we'd need several more hours at least to talk you into it. And wait for you to check your spreadsheet."

"I did, too," Carrie said, and she lifted her glass. "Here's to turning a new corner, and seeing what's on the other side."

Faith laughed, and knew they were right. This wasn't like her—not how she'd normally behave—but when you knew something was right, and smart, you just had to stick your neck out.

And that felt good, and right. And she knew that whatever happened, she'd be all right with her best friends by her side.

I hope you enjoyed A Newport Sunrise!

Look for the next book, available for pre-order:

A Newport Christmas

If you'd like to receive an email when my next book releases, please join my mailing list